How Hamisu Survived Bad Kidneys and a Bad Son-in-Law

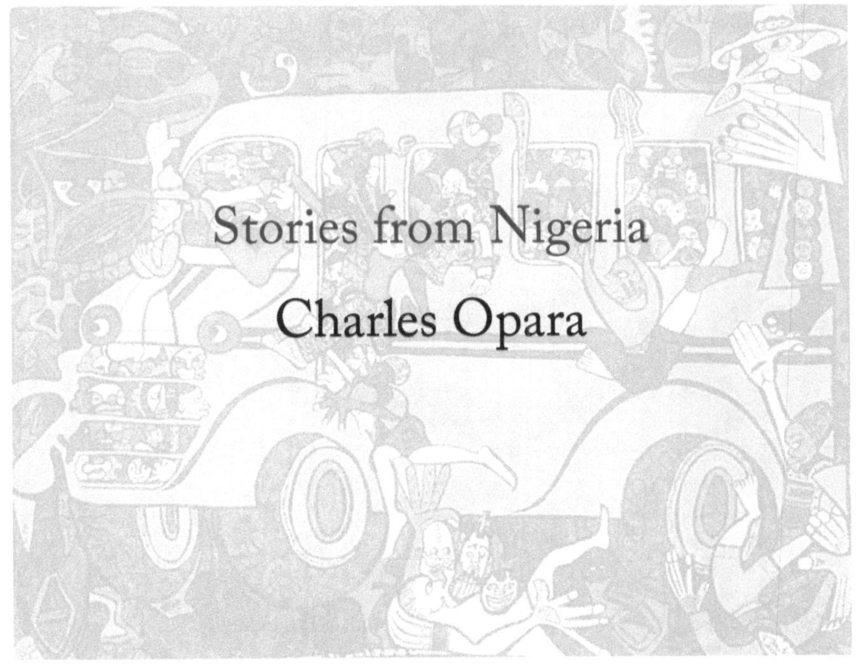

Fomite
Burlington, VT

ISBN: 978-1-953236-23-4
Library of Congress Control Number: 2021934691

Fomite
58 Peru Street
Burlington, VT 05401
www.fomitepress.com

Contents

THE DREAM

1.

IN A SOCCER STADIUM, they would have called it a Mexican wave, but here it looks like a staging of Moses parting the Red Sea, a sort of thaumaturgy—a preacher is running through crowds, tapping heads, and tumping over bodies. It's a Christian prayer night, a church-sponsored telecast Bob-Manuel would normally switch off, but instead is fully absorbed in, so absorbed he doesn't hear the rap on his door. He stares at the images of the sick rolling on the floor and recovering (from the floor), teary-eyed as they shout churchy vernacular in the aftermath of a simple but traumatizing tactile gesture, and hesitates when he glimpses a form in his visitor's chair. It's Mr. Sokari from the accounting department. His guest had let himself in and chosen not to distract him. As they listen to one incredible story of healing after another, Bob-Manuel laments how politicians, church ministers, and visa lottery agents were always cashing in on the hopes of the masses.

"We are superstitious by nature, you know how we are. We easily self-delude," Bob-Manuel says to his guest.

"We?" Mr. Sokari asks.

"Africans," Bob-Manuel says, leaning back in his chair so he can fix his gaze on Mr. Sokari.

"So you're saying this is superstition at work?"

"I'm saying this is an elocutionist-slash-illusionist taking advantage of ignorant people. The simple placing of his hand on their heads has a placebo effect on their minds. And he even has a name for it: faith."

Bob-Manuel doesn't like preachers very much. He blames them for job losses in psychology. In his part of the world, many would rather go to them to discuss their problems than come to a trained psychologist like him. But that aside. Right now it's time for him to listen to Mr. Sokari complain about his boss for the drive-me-crazieth time. He knows his clients find his attention therapeutic, just as others find the same in the touch of a faith healer.

Mr. Sokari fills Bob-Manuel in on the latest in his feud with his boss, Shalom Ogaga, an unmarried woman pushing forty. "Women get like that when they are that age and still single," he says. "You see, my bachelor friend, the union of marriage triggers spurts of growth in a couple. The man is responsible for the increase in rationality in his partner and has her to thank for his improved emotionality. That's how they complement each other. And that's why a woman's reasoning faculty never learns to walk without the help of a man, no matter her age. The sad thing is, That Woman thinks she's a devout Christian, but she's a godless, loveless she-devil."

Still speaking as the expert, he explains That Woman's temple lifestyle:

"You don't have to be psychic to know she's praying for a husband. But if God were to answer her prayer, wouldn't He be ruining the life of some unfortunate guy?"

Bob-Manuel blames Shalom's testiness on the post-menopausal emotions of an ascetic, a woman now angry with herself for having guarded her buried treasure (buried old treasure, is what it is now) hoping to gift it to a spouse with a one-word interjection that translates 'because you deserve this', Wah-la, a woman who has gone from feeling like a nymph to feeling like a laughingstock, gone from being chased to just being chaste, all because she waited so goddamn long to have goddamn…

"Sex?" Mr. Sokari finishes, leaning forward, a light-bulb expression in his eyes. "Are you saying she needs… sex?"

"I'm saying she needs therapy, not a church sermon. It's what I've been saying all along. She might find men threatening and feel the need to go on the offensive. Believe me, her social skills would benefit more from an evening dinner party than an all-night prayer vigil. She's the one who ought to be coming to see me for counselling, but those preachers are keeping her deluded."

His utterance draws a snicker from his guest who reminds him his door says 'Assistant Head of Human Resources' and only a handful of people know he's a psychologist.

"I only found out at last year's end-of-year party," Mr. Sokari says, "when you joked that you might have started a Ponzi scheme if your masters in occupational psychology hadn't gotten you this job."

"Organizational psychology," Bob-Manuel corrects. And he wasn't joking. To avoid competing for clients with pastors, imams, priests, Niger-Delta militants, and other clerics, Bob-Manuel had specialized in organizational psychology and applied for the position of assistant head of H.R. at Shell Petroleum Nigeria. The rest is history. The company now pays him a gallant sum to shuffle papers around, nothing related to the practice.

"How would you like to go on a date?"

The question catches Bob-Manuel in the face like a long arc of piss he had seen rising in the air but hadn't thought would swing his way. "With whom?" he asks, feeling foolish.

"Her," Mr. Sokari confirms.

Bob-Manuel is amused at how Shalom has gone from 'That Woman' to 'Her'. "You can't be serious," he says.

"But I am. And why not? There is no Mrs. Effiong-Bassey in the picture, as far as I can tell."

Bob-Manuel tries to refuse. He goes from asserting 'I won't do it' to suggesting she might find it insulting: him trying to match-make her, to pleading 'Please, I'm a professional; that's not how I operate.'

"I'm only asking you to be her friend and listen to her as a friend, and then advise her as a psychologist. Prove to me that psychology works." It's a challenge Bob-Manuel finds hard to turn down. "Alright," he says. "But it doesn't have to be a date. I could attend her church and when she sees me there, a familiar face from work, we could strike up a conversation."

That's fine by me," Mr. Sokari says.

AND SO, FOR THE NEXT THREE MONTHS, Bob-Manuel becomes a regular at Living Word Gospel, That Woman's Christian community. Their first meeting goes better than planned. She asks him to give his life to God, and he tells her that if she looked around, she would see that there was life outside the church. She gives in to him, and after three months, they—marry. It's not the turn of events Bob-Manuel had foreseen, but these things happen. Yes, it may not have solved Mr. Sokari's problem, but it certainly lessened it: he never again had to travel three blocks (and five floors) to Bob-Manuel's office to complain about That Woman. He did it in the next block. He was wrong about one thing, though: Shalom wasn't 'pushing forty', she was forty-two.

Shalom is as assertive as only an only child can be. She's used to having things her way and when she doesn't, she's edgy and can be blunt, insolently blunt. With her, tantrums are frequent, and if you come at her, you are the bully, not her; you're the one who doesn't know that deferring to a woman is the mark of maturity in a man.

She's perceptive. Some of the things she said about Mr. Sokari were spot on; she described him as an insecure little boy, a self-absorbed egotist who constantly needed the reassuring of others to manage his frail ego.

From his encounter with Shalom, Bob-Manuel decides never to conclude until he has heard both sides of the story.

2.

Bob-Manuel and Shalom go from a family of two to a family of four in five years. Every Sunday, they sit with their daughters Ruth and Deborah in the fifth pew of the leftmost section of Living Word Gospel. Bob-Manuel likes the seat close to the standing fan in the middle of the aisle where he usually catches a nap during the sermon.

Sunday is the family-outing day, and starting with Sunday service, he hopes a room full of strangers will turn all four of them into a chain of paper-dolls, in the figurative sense. Be it a theatre or a restaurant, even the places where people call you 'brother', finding yourself in a crowd has a way of infusing a stronger sense of kin. Perhaps not today. He's not feeling that bond just yet, not with Shalom nodding to the minister's argument that there's no salvation for suicides. How can she support talk like that? And what is this public speaker trying to start? More resentment? More frustration? The World Pro-Suicide Day?

"Uplifting words for anyone who has lost someone with a death wish," Bob-Manuel whispers to Shalom, a solemn member of the congregation. He manages to chip in 'See why they should never replace us?' before she swats him away with her hand fan.

When Bob-Manuel was promoted to the head of H.R., Shalom was so ecstatic that she gave a testimony in church. The testimony was okay; it was the donation she wanted to make that Bob-Manuel didn't like.

"Can't you see?" he said. "I've made it despite them. There is no way in hell I'm giving them any part of my salary."

"Give your life to God," Shalom said, and he retorted, "Yes, we should do just that: give Him our lives, not our money or our sound minds."

Pause for a moment. Before you judge Bob-Manuel, consider this: he lives in a country where swindlers masquerade as men of God, a country where you'll find some of the richest church ministers in the world. So. Can you honestly blame him for feeling fraud-proof and a lot wiser than most?

Bob-Manuel is brought back from his reverie by a slap. In hindsight, it started as pats on the cheek that grew in urgency and intensity. It's Ruth. She's standing in a forest of bodies, a watchful Shalom towering over her. The sermon has ended and Ruth, encouraged by Shalom, from the look of it, wants him to stand up and join the praise and worship.

3.

Bob-Manual is filing memos, one morning, when Mr. Ibimina Tubo -Tamuno barges into his office with a story he thought of sharing because it supports Bob-Manuel's opinion that church ministers are bigger menaces than blessings. He narrates how his steward's twelve-year-old son returned home much worse than he left, after spending months in the care of a faith healer. The boy was rushed to a clinic where his condition was diagnosed as ADHD. Unfortunately, he developed other mental complications while he was there.

"His parents should sue," Bob-Manuel says.

Mr. Ibimina sighs. "They have no money. I considered footing the bill myself, but after discussing it with my wife and discovering that the man in question was Reverend Light Wambebe, the founder of The Church of New Creations, I thought it best to let God be the judge."

Bob-Manuel hisses, irritated by his guest's undisguised admiration for the faith healer. He wants to educate the sheep sitting in his visitor's chair—the mental slave still living in a time when an eclipse would have been a sign of the Last Day and a weatherman would have been a prophet—but decides against it. He offers to sponsor the legal action.

"You would do that?" Mr. Ibimina asks.

"Why not? A professional would lose his license for doing a thing like that. Why should it be different for church ministers? Go tell your steward that he will get justice for what was done to his son."

Later that day, Bob-Manuel gets a call. It's Mr. Ibimina. He informs him that the boy's father is not keen on the idea: "He now believes that whatever Reverend Light had done to his son had worked because before now, when he told the boy to stop doing that, he did it more, but now he does nothing."

"Tell him that if we win, the court will make the pastor pay him millions of naira in damages," Bob-Manuel says. "Tell him that I know we will win."

Bob-Manuel holds the line while the blur of a conversation goes on at the other end. After roughly a minute, Mr. Ibimina speaks into his mouthpiece. "That settles it then," he says.

When Shalom returns home, Bob-Manuel shares the details of his day at work, how he plans to sue a faith healer who turned a little boy with an alphabet disease into a cabbage. She says the word is 'vegetable' and that he has all her support, but right now, she needs him to shut the toilet door so she can do her business in peace.

Next, he visits his old college mate, Arinze Wokedi, a lawyer with whom he had studied law before flunking into psychology, deemed cognate and lower in prestige.

"Did you say 'Reverend Light Wambebe'?" Arinze asks, his eyes half-closed in thought. "Isn't he the popular TV minister who drives demons out of people by felling them like trees?"

"He's the one." Bob-Manuel nods.

"His sponsored programs are on every TV station. How much do you think they cost? This case will be huge. That man is loaded."

4.

Bob-Manuel has a plan. If it works, it will make him a key witness in the trial. He will visit the unsuspecting faith healer and claim he suffers from sporadic demonic attacks and experience his aboriginal methods, first-hand.

It takes two weeks, and a ridiculous sum, from the day he books his appointment to the day of his appointment. When he finally meets Reverend Light Wambebe, he's a little nettled by his fresh face and bright eyes. The man is fair-complexioned, middle-aged, no more than forty-five, plump, oozing with the goodness of the Good News and the Good Life, what it must mean to 'become a CONC (Church Of New Creations) Christian today' as his billboards stress. He has an air Bob-Manuel doesn't like. It's partly the way he removes his eyes after sizing you and the way he raises his hand to hush his subordinates, the way he always has at least one subordinate around him wherever he goes.

Bob-Manuel states his name, his age, and his profession for the reverend and a slim, bespectacled understudy.

"What is it you want God to help you with?" the understudy asks him.

"I have trouble focusing on things that don't interest me, even when I know they should," Bob-Manuel says. "I try, but my mind keeps wandering."

"What sort of things?" the understudy asks.

Distracted by the notes the reverend is making, Bob-Manuel says, "Sorry. But what things are you referring to?"

"The things that don't interest you. Even though they should."

"Oh. Those things. Well… How do I put it? They are the things I'm doing while I'm thinking about other things I plan to do."

"What are those things?"

"And what things are we talking about now? The things that lead to the other things or the other things?"

"The things that lead to the other things," the understudy says, getting irritated. But his efforts only make Bob-Manuel say one thing after another. The reverend stops his scribbling and takes over the questioning.

Bob-Manuel tells him how his mind keeps wandering off whenever he tries to read the Bible or listen in church. The reverend and the understudy exchange glances. Bingo, their eyes say.

"Where does your mind wander off to, most times?" the reverend asks.

Bob-Manuel is tempted to make something up, like waking up in a mermaid kingdom, but he resists the urge. "The last time it happened," he says, "I was thinking of how I could turn someone's misfortune into profit for both of us. You know how it is with this and that. That kind of stuff."

"Ah," the understudy says, bobbing his head, "This or that, and that kind of stuff."

"Exactly," Bob-Manuel says, head-bobbing along. The reverend scribbles.

Bob-Manuel's hosts mutter to each other and hand him a copy of the Bible. They give him verses to read out loud and when he's done, they take back the Bible and ask, "The scripture you just read, what book was it taken from?"

Bob-Manuel can't remember. One of Paul's letters, he thinks, Galatians or Caucasians.

"What did it say?"

Well... um... Paul was telling the people to.... to give their lives to God.

They stare at him, looking confused themselves. It isn't the answer they're looking for. (Is a slam-dunk still a slam-dunk if you bring down the net?)

At the end of the session, the reverend says, "You are always distracted because you like to fantasize about a different life. And the reason for this is, you find your job unfulfilling and think you deserve better, think you deserve to be in a line of work that utilizes your skills. You are not satisfied with just earning a salary; you want to earn respect too. In other words, you want more recognition than you currently have. And this preoccupies you so much that it's hard for you to focus on anything else. I recommend you pray and meditate often; busy yourself with spiritual things."

Bob-Manuel is speechless. It feels like a clinical psychologist has just psychoanalyzed him. There is nothing dilettante about the reverend's words. In fact, they made sense.

"You are not going to cast out my devil?" Bob-Manuel asks.

The reverend shakes his head. "It is better to learn how to overcome him yourself so you can defeat him whenever he tries to reach you. The type of devil you have is lazy, wishful, and looking for admirers."

Bob-Manuel cannot believe his ears. It is not funny when the tables are turned and you are forced to admire the ironies of life. Who is the trained expert here? Is the devil now another name for a vice? Can that hold in court? What happened to the traditionalist view of a unique existence that takes over lives and needs to be exorcized?

He concludes that the reverend has an inferiority complex and doesn't want to be stereotyped. Yes, that's it. The man is pretending to be an intellectual because he knows he's dealing with one.

5.

TRYING TO FIND EVIDENCE to use against the reverend has left Bob-Manuel a little disoriented. Only the sight of his Toyota Land Cruiser makes him realize why he's roaming about the parking lot. He reaches into his pocket and pulls out his car key, but he doesn't notice his wallet slipping and falling to the ground. A scruffy-looking man picks it up and calls to him. "Mister, Mister," he yells. Bob-Manuel turns to look, but all he sees is a beggar audacious enough to call him from a distance. He ignores the idiot and gets into his car.

"Sir, you dropped your wallet," the beggar shouts.

True enough, the man is waving Bob-Manuel's wallet in the air. Bob-Manuel kills the engine and beckons the beggarly man over. The man comes up to his car window and hands him his wallet. Bob-Manuel opens his wallet, takes out a one-thousand-naira note, and offers it to the man. To his shock, the man turns it down.

Bob-Manuel takes out another one-thousand naira note. "How is this?" he asks. "Large enough now?"

"Thank you, sir, but I don't want your money," the man says. "Just ask God to bless me for returning your wallet the next time you pray."

Bob-Manuel's eyebrows stay raised. He cannot believe his ears. Are the homeless now turning down money—two grand? "What is your problem?" he says to the man. "Is two thousand naira not good enough for you? Here. Take it and buy soap."

Bob-Manuel's words put welts in the man's eyes. For a whole minute, he stands there with Bob-Manuel's banknotes flapping in his face. "Sir," he says. "I have been fasting and praying for six days. Please keep your money. If I wanted money, certainly not from a man like you."

"Now we are getting somewhere." Bob-Manuel steps out of his car and bangs the door. "What do you mean by a man like me?"

"Men who look down on others."

"Oh? So I am looking down on you by offering you a reward? It's not your fault. You haven't starved enough. Wretch!"

Pause for a second. Before you judge Bob-Manuel, consider this: He has just come from a counseling session where he was labeled a sad, frustrated, insignificant man trying to prove his worth by undermining others, a fire fueled by the devil... Okay. So maybe he thinks it was implied. Still, it was the reverend who put those thoughts there. He was the one who uncapped the keg and left it open for air to sour the palm wine. Well, now Bob-Manuel no longer wants to play the mumu to men who act holier-than-thou.

There is more. The beggarly man is clearly in the early stages of mental decline: denial. Any psychologist would see the signs: a shabby appearance and an ego yet to take a dive. Unfortunately for this man, who should be in an institution and not a prayer house, he is getting in the way of the wall Bob-Manuel so badly wants to punch.

Bob-Manuel and the man exchange words. They raise their voices at each other. A small crowd comes between them. One of the interveners asks what the matter is.

"I offer him money for finding my wallet and he says he doesn't take money from people like me," Bob-Manuel says.

"He insulted me first," the man yells. "What is wrong with asking him to keep his money? Why must he say I should take it and buy soap?"

Between sobs, the now regretful do-gooder explains to the crowd how the whole thing started. He's not the same man who was acting all dignified and superior. Bob-Manuel is happy at this. The more he looks at him, a believer trying to live the monastic life, the more he sees the similarity between religion, extreme poverty, and cerebral malaria: they all mess with your mind. Shalom fasts too. She says it helps build her spiritual stamina so she can withstand temptation, but all it does is put her in a foul mood. Like this man here.

"I'm sorry," Bob-Manuel says to the monastic man. "I was completely out of line. I'm having a bad day."

The matter is settled. They shake hands and everyone is happy. One of those who intervened, a thin elderly man with an Adam's Apple the size of a child's scrotum, blames the escalation of the whole incident on the monastic man for not accepting the money. He should have taken the cash and put it in the petition box with a prayer for God to bless Bob-Manuel. He offers to receive the money on the monastic man's behalf to do just that. Clever man, Bob-Manuel thinks. He hadn't seen where the old man's speech was leading and had even been nodding the whole time. Now he just wants to applaud. He backs away and scoffs in the man's face, laughing in crescendos until his cackles say the words he does not say.

6.

THAT NIGHT, BOB-MANUEL WOKE UP in a construction site, someplace with men on scaffolds around a tall building unlike any he'd seen. The building could pass for a skyscraper, except the only structure on it were rungs—it had no floors and no rooms. So it was a tower, a watchtower, it seemed. There were no Caterpillars, tractors, or any kind of machine. All the workers had were diggers, hammers, chisels, and wheelbarrows. He was in a group that smashed rocks and handed them to another group that carried them off in wheelbarrows. His co-workers were grotesque—they were hideous, to be honest. Their bodies were young and strong, but strange enough, their faces had grown simian with age: elastic skins over deep-set eyes; shrunken noses with nostrils that stared at you like a pair of eyes; and longer-than-normal extensions between their noses and upper lips. Their hands and feet were dry and wrinkled, and they had nails you only saw on those old enough to hear their deathbeds calling. They sounded sick from the way they wheezed and coughed. And when they bared their teeth, they showed pink upper gums and missing teeth. Fights broke out often. Sometimes, someone was killed.

Where the hell was he? He asked one of the men why they were building the tower and the man said, "We want to see God so we can plead our cases, face-to-face."

It came as a relief when he was asked to leave: he didn't belong there, they said. And after checking his reflection in a lake and seeing he was still himself, he couldn't agree more. Thank God.

After travelling many miles, he found a settlement with people who looked a lot more like him. He was grateful too that they were making a cooking fire because he hadn't eaten for days. Things went well for a while. The people were welcoming. They shared some of the things they had and stood up for each other, some of the time. But they had a flaw. They were volatile; they blew up over the smallest things. They were clearly smarter than those he left at the construction site but emotionally, they had room to grow. Tired of always being afraid of what he might say or do to upset the next person, he packed some grains of rice and left the settlement.

He journeyed over savannahs and open plains, where the grasses grew greener and taller until it bloomed into a tropical paradise: a garden with fountains, fruit trees, and waterfalls. He could not believe his eyes when he saw that the people there were all young—they showed no signs of decrepitude—all healthy, and all beautiful, very beautiful. They didn't need to sleep in houses because there were no mosquitoes or animals or bad weather to harm them. They shared everything they had and were always ready to make sacrifices for whomever. They listened to each other and were happy all the time. They had no worries. Farming was a waste of energy because all kinds of crops, from wheat plants to fruit trees, grew readily from the ground. All they had to do was pick them and cook them if they needed that. They were great cooks. The air always smelled of nice things like Oha Soup and White Soup. No-one sold or bought anything; everything was free. And no-one ever lacked anything or had more than enough. The only work they did was cooking, making clothes (splendid garments Shalom would love), and cleaning themselves and their surroundings.

Strange as all this was, it seemed genuine. But to be sure, when a fair-skinned nymphet offered him a bouquet, he threw it to the ground and jumped all over it with both feet, and then waited to see her reaction. She stared at him, looking as though he had shot her through the heart. He could tell she had never seen such violence in her life, such wanton behavior, what manner of man would stamp on petunias? He smiled as he watched her in a muse, trying to imagine what her expression would be if he took a leap from a flower destroyer to a virgin deflowerer, beautiful as she was. Frightened, the girl ran away, shivering and muffling back tears as if wailing was another form of violence.

"Come back," he called after her. "I was only testing you." And then he remembered: no-one shouts here. They only raised their voices to sing and, Lord, could they sing.

The girl didn't return. Yes, he did feel a little mean but honestly, it didn't bother him much. The people here were forgiving. They were like puppies: they always took you back. If he were a bad person, all he had to do was slap one of them and they would all obey him.

A sudden spell of dizziness came over him and he fell to the grass. When he woke up, he was back at the settlement, back with the volatile people, back with the not-so-ugly and the not-so-beautiful.

"No," he screamed."God, please, take me back. I was only checking. I was checking to see if…"

Wait... What is this? The not-so-pretty woman beside him is— Shalom.

"Hush, dear, you had a nightmare," she says. "You can relax. You're with me now."

"Oh thank goodness," he says. "So I'm not dead?"

"Not yet."

"I dreamt that I went to three different places. The first was—"

"Shh. Go back to sleep. We have work tomorrow. You can tell me all about it in the morning. Or better yet, after work." She slumps back on the bed, rolls to one side, and with a sigh, drags the bed covers over her.

7.

Bob-Manuel and Shalom are standing in front of the mirror, brushing their teeth when Bob-Manuel asks, "Honey, am I a good person?"

Shalom gargles and spits into the sink. She studies him through the mirror and says, "It's not enough to be a good person, I keep telling you that. You need to be a God person. Good people don't survive severe tests. They don't have strong enough roots, that's why. Trauma can make them despair and take their lives."

"But I believe in God. On top of that, I do things for people. I fight their fights. I even pay for their litigations. What more can you ask?"

"About that," Shalom says. "I think it's funny that you're making such a big sacrifice for a boy that you've never gone to see."

Bob-Manuel rinses his mouth. "You're right," he says. "I should visit. I know what I'll do. I'll follow Mr. Ibimina home from work today and see the boy for myself."

"Good idea."

8.

AT THE CLOSE OF WORK, Bob-Manuel finds Mr. Ibimina waiting for him in the parking lot as they agreed. They get into their cars and join a line of other cars advancing through the security post at the gate. Bob-Manuel tails Mr. Ibimina to his house. At the Tubo-Tamuno residence, he's greeted by the missis, has a few shots of Dom Pérignon, eats some peppered fish, tells a few anecdotes to the keen couple, but he almost chokes on a fishbone when he learns from the missis that Reverend Light is there too. "He's in the Boys' Quarters attending to the boy as we speak," she says.

Reverend Light Wambebe? Here? "How long has this been going on?" Bob-Manuel asks.

"It's his third visit," Mr. Ibimina replies.

"What?" Bob-Manuels shrieks. "I would have thought the boy's father would not want anything to do with him, let alone allow him near his son, after what happened. But how could you, Mr. Ibimina? How could you invite him into your home? This is a man we're planning to sue. Do you realize how this could hurt our case?"

Mr. Ibimina and the Missis glance at each other. The Missis gets up and leaves. "I've been trying to tell you," Mr. Ibimina says, "the boy is getting better. His father doesn't want to press charges anymore."

"Cowards. We'll be suing an impostor, not desecrating King Jaja of Opobo. The man is a fraud, and you know it."

Mr. Ibimina downs his last swallow of Dom Perignon and sits back in his chair."My wife has been promoted ever since he taught us how to pray."

"Your wife was due for a promotion, was she not?" "Yes, but—"

"Why do you people magnify mere coincidences? Because you are men of small minds, that's why. Anyway, I didn't come here to fight. I came to see the boy."

"Let me go and see if the reverend is done," Mr. Ibimina says. "It will not be nice to interrupt him."

Bob-Manuel cannot believe the insult. There he is, in the home of a man who sees him for the expert he is, and yet this same man is making him dance Eregbu to the reverend's music.

Mr. Ibimina disappears behind satin curtains, leaving Bob-Manuel alone with his family portraits crowding the walls and staring him down. A short while later, he returns with the boy, his father, the reverend, and that same understudy.

"We meet again, brother," the understudy says. "Hope you have been praying and reading your Bible."

Bob-Manuel brushes past him and stops at the boy. He has seen more pleasant-looking boys. This one is about twelve, is thin and rather sickly-looking. He has no drooling look so that should mean no autism. He has a rather awkward-looking head, bean-shaped and seemingly compressed at the sides. Not to worry. Puberty should take care of that. He checks the boy's reflexes. They're good.

"I need some time alone with him," Bob-Manuel says to the boy's father, a short man in a browning white singlet.

"His mind used to wander like yours," the reverend says to Bob-Manuel. "You have the more advanced stage of his condition."

Pause for a bit. Let's analyze what's at play here. Before you blame Bob-Manuel for what is about to happen try to appreciate the aggravation he faces. He's at a friend's home to see a sick boy, a therapist making a house call, and this… this con artist is belittling him in front of his hosts all because, two days ago, he pretended to seek his counsel.

Mr. Ibimina gawks at Bob-Manuel. "You know each other?" He turns to the reverend. "Have you treated him before?"

"Yes," the understudy says."He came in for counselling on Tuesday."

Bob-Manuel snorts. "I won't exactly say I was 'treated'. I was only checking to see if…"

Wait… His words strike him as strangely familiar. They're the words from his dream. The coincidence shames him like a cockcrow after a betrayal. He quickly changes the subject.

"Tell me, Reverend," he says. "If my case is so similar to the boy's, then why did you deal with us differently? Is it because he's a child that you think you can get away with abusing him?"

"Excuse me?" the understudy blurts like someone who has just heard his name. He sees his master's raised hand and steps back.

"Who said I abused him?" the reverend asks.

Bob-Manuel doesn't answer. He hopes Mr. Ibimina and the boy's father will attest to it, but no-one utters a word.

"I see," the reverend says. "You think you are the technocrat here. But what you don't know is, what you see is what you want to see. It's what you want to believe."

Bob-Manuel laughs to ascend to the condescending. "The boy came back from your house worse than he left. He doesn't have a devil in him; he was diagnosed with a known medical condition. But what do you care? If you don't see devils in people, how will you make money?"

The understudy curses and the reverend cautions him.

"I know I may seem foolish to you, even paranoid," the reverend says, "but it's nothing new. Some people think the whole point of their existence is to live, procreate, and die. But somewhere deep within, even they know there is more to them than what their five senses can perceive. There is a voice within each one of us that alerts us to our true calling. And this is not science fiction, no. It's prescience. An inborn intuition of our intangible source. I only hope that when they realize that returning to this source is the whole point, it won't be too late."

"Mr. Elocutionist," Bob-Manuel says. "I know what's real and what's not, thank you. And I know you are a fake. So stop distracting me. And stop speaking in that magisterial tone. If you're so good at what you do, how come the boy is worse?"

"He's getting better," Mr. Ibimina says. "How many times must I tell you?"

The boy's father nods.

Bob-Manuel is feeling outnumbered, but he's not about to be intimidated by this churchman and his newfound congregation. "Tell me how you cured him," he says to the reverend.

"I helped him find inner peace," the reverend says. "He resisted, at first, but in the end, he was so overwhelmed with grief that he collapsed on the ground and fell apart. And as we all know, after a tumult comes a calm. He has woken up to a new reality. He is at peace with himself now. And as a result, he is more focused."

"You lie."

"You need that peace too."

"I need you to stop playing mind games and tell me the truth."

"You are choosing to bury the voices that tell you what you don't want to accept beneath those that tell you what you want to hear. Silence the voices in your head and discover the peace that eludes you. Come into the truth. Stop fighting it."

"Enough of your babbles and your inflicted sense of self-importance." But Bob-Manuel is hearing his own inflicted sense of self-importance.

"Mr. Psychologist, one of you needs to decrease so the other can increase."

"You are mad."

"Which voice will you listen to? Flesh or spirit? Desire or design? Temporal or eternal? Choose."

"Now I see you have lost it."

"By your own admission, you have managed to become a success despite your absent-mindedness, your habitual dreaminess. So tell me, why are you unhappy?"

"By my own admission? What are you talking about?"

"You said when you were kicked out of law school, your father made you work in a construction site so you would appreciate where people with no college degree end up. You said the lesson you learned was, failures get pushed around. Invariably, you would think… successes are adored. You want to be adored, Mr. Psychologist."

"That's just common sense. Everybody wants to be adored."

"If you become obsessed with that thought, you will see those around you as adorers and potential adorers."

"Keep your philosophies to yourself. If I let you go on, all you'll be doing is making up stories."

"I am only trying to show you the other side of the story, the one you are refusing to see."

Bob-Manuel remembers how hearing Shalom's take on Mr. Sokari, a former disciple, had made him vow never to jump to conclusions until he had heard both sides of the story. He wonders why this thought is coming to him now. He shrugs off the self-incriminating voices in his head and stomps to the foyer to collect his coat.

In the foyer, behind the veil of the satin curtain, he takes one last look at the one he lost...

My Life in Lekki Montana

Jooji. Jooji Jemedafe. (Joo-jee Je-may-dah-fay.) My inner child sings when I say her name. She's always warm with me, extending more than what I would call common courtesy, but she's never once said my name. Think she's forgotten it. But that's okay. Glad she's not stuck-up like some of the other mothers. She works, that's probably why. I hear she teaches home economics at Queen's College, where she did her youth service. At least she's not a house-sitting homemaker like most of us. Good for her: she doesn't share our need to put up a front to hide our insecurities. Tom said his friends' wives were the way they were because it's how his friends like them: exotic and feisty (if you agree feistiness in a woman means having a mind of her own). He said his friends have a predilection for foreign things and foreign ways, anything that says 'pricy and extremely rare'— and it's the same with them when it comes to wives and pets: they like the expensive, dangerous breeds because they think it underlines their social class and because they think they'll impress with their ability to domesticate. And unless I become like that, he said, I'll always seem to them like someone who lacks sophistication, someone whose humble background still shows and not someone in their league. And if I ever become like that, he added with an air of finality, I won't be the same person he took to the altar.

Tom and I got married last year and moved to Lekki Montana, a gated community in the Lekki area of Lagos Peninsula. (I hear the name 'Montana' was taken from the hit country song 'Meet me in Montana' by Dan Seals. In the song, Montana was a place where dreams were preserved.) I was forty-three when I got married, an old bride, to put it bluntly. Believe it or not, it was my first serious relationship. I guess I should count myself lucky, considering the marriage prospects for women my age. It's a surprise I got married at all. I never dreamed of becoming a wife, never fantasized about my wedding day like many teenage girls. Moreover, I was never envious of my friends when they tied the knot, partly because I couldn't see myself putting up with some of the sexists they married, forgetting I was nearing my forties, well past my prime and the vantage that afforded me a choice in men.

I don't envy Jooji—I might wish I were her, but I don't feel resentful that I'm not. No resentment here. Her husband is a renowned heart surgeon and a fine specimen of a man, but that's not why I might wish I were her. Hardly. I like her for always looking stunning, and for always looking like she's having the time of her life. Whenever she walks in late to a PTA meeting, everyone takes notice. I love how she carries herself, how she seems to view those around her. If you don't like her, it's probably because you're jealous and don't want to. She's a woman with grace and style (she's the real deal, Sister), and she's humble about it too, she's humble and polite without trying hard to please. And that's how you should keep it in Lekki Montana.

Over here, the word for those who try hard to please is 'obedient', and you should only use that word to describe your house help or your child. Or your wife, if you're a sadomasochist or just a plain old-fashioned male chauvinist. Again, when you're nice, people think you're slavish, think you're meant for ordering around like a KFC burger. I can't say I have friends here. If I did, they would probably be not- nice. I don't want to do like they do, but I'm learning to fight with my air of confidence and my sarcasm. Somehow Jooji rises above all that. And that's why I want to be her friend.

I look forward to running into her, whenever I can. We normally meet at the local supermarket or the members-only tennis club. Or at George's school. I didn't run into her today, but that's okay. There's always tomorrow.

George asks me if I could just stay in the van whenever I come to pick him. My initial thoughts are, Woah. That came out of nowhere. But why not? I would be happy to pick him from school by way of a drive-through, every single time. Wouldn't that make things easier for me? But I sense there's more to his request, something more than his seemingly selfless desire to help me out, a point he's yet to get to. And I sense, too, that he wants me to ask so he can tell me what it is. So I ask. "Because everyone will think you're my mom." And when I don't ask what's wrong with that, he does me the favour: "Don't want people thinkin' you're my mom."

Otito diri Jesu! Thank God I no be ya mama. The brat is testing my patience. No. You won't come down to his level, I tell myself to calm myself. If you let them swing you around, you'll lose the rally—the words of my tennis coach; when they go lower, you go higher, thank you, Michelle Obama.

I tell him that if he asks politely, I just might do that. I tell him this in Queen's English. I try to speak to him in Queen's English because he spent most of his life with his mum in London. And because speaking with this accent makes me feel a rank higher—he speaks in the Cockney dialect—makes me feel less like his nanny (I've never admitted that to myself until now). But Pidgin tinged with Igbo is the language of my impulse, the language of my insults—what I tend to utter when I'm not feeling very elegant—a habit I've been trying to kick ever since I came here. I guess it's my default mode.

"But I was polite," George protests.

"No. You were rude. You were curt." I know he doesn't know what 'curt' means, but he knows it's his cue to apologize. "George? What do you say to me?"

"Leave me alone."

'Kids'.

That's all Tom says when we get home and I tell him what George said to me on our way back from school. He makes George apologize and that's that. No pep talk. He doesn't explain why he shouldn't be so blunt. My God. Thomas Daramola Alakija! Is this how you want to raise your son? Tom thinks we should be patient with him: he's still dealing with being separated from his mother. I think Tom tries too hard to win his affection, so hard he forgets to be a father; he's more like a grandfather if you ask me: too lenient. George is a child from his philandering past, a secret he kept from his ex for twelve years. George came to live with us two months ago, the boy's mother's idea, Tom had said. Tom's always making excuses for people. He tolerates this and extenuates that. I think he gets it from trading in used cars, he owns a car dealership in Opebi-Allen. It's frustrating, sometimes. Why do I always have to be the bigger man? It's not always about George. There's Tom's sisters. His friend's wives. And the list goes on.

Tom is a good man, I know that. He's kind, considerate, thoughtful, experienced, and wise. He's almost seventy and is now above being petty or having poor judgement, unlike his friends, most of whom are ten years younger and don't know how old he is, thanks to his pudginess and baby face. I get the sense he has a better grasp of beauty—of true beauty—the kind you can't see with your eyes. You might think this is a good thing. But when you start to wonder if he finds you attractive or even sees you, you start to feel alone. I wish he were more spontaneous, more concerned about the things I'm concerned about.

When I heard Jooji had resigned from her job and started a daycare in our community, I was happy for her. Her school is the latest hotspot. I hear residents are enrolling their babies and toddlers by the dozen. I imagine her likeability must have helped, her beauty too. (Aren't children just drawn to beautiful people? I know I was, especially women.) And she's a good role model too, even for adults. From all the talk going around, I learn she's looking to hire nannies for her daycare. I consider it. Why not? It will give me a reason to leave the house more. And a chance to get close to her.

I DRIVE TO HER HOME, the next morning, and I'm met at the door by one of her nannies, a woman I think I've been introduced to, her sister-in-law, if I'm not mistaken. The woman sees I haven't brought a child and assumes I'm there to see Jooji. "Come in. She's in the kitchen," she says over the noise of two babies crying in their prams. From the position of the prams (near the entrance), it appears their mothers have just dropped them off and they're yet to be attended to.

Jooji's house has the same design as mine—we both live in 21st-century craftsman bungalows—so I know my way around. The living room has a large playpen for toddlers, to protect them from being pushed to the ground by the older, more-rambunctious kids, who are chasing each other around a sofa instead of watching Teletubbies like the rest.

In the kitchen, I find Jooji in the cold section. She's at a table with another woman, not a kitchen table, but a dining table for two. (Tom and I have one like it we use outdoors, except hers has stools instead of chairs, and it's made of wood.) I think it's dainty. I love the way it's beautifully carved like a chess piece. My host smiles when she sees me. She signals 'I'll be with you in a sec' so I find a spot next to the French-door refrigerator and wait. I like her kitchen. It's well organized and spacey. While I wait, I listen to their conversation: there's nothing else to listen to but the fridge. She's interviewing for the position of 'a teacher's assistant', that's what she calls it. The applicant, who says she's also a college applicant gets the job, even after she palters around a question and is forced to admit she hasn't had any experience with infants.

"Sorry for keeping you waiting," Jooji says to me when it's over, inviting me to the seat next to hers with a hand gesture.

"No apology needed," I say. "I love how you've turned your parlor into a daycare."

"Oh. Thank you. You should see my guest bedroom; it's a nursery now."

"I can tell you're good with kids."

"I try. I have three, but I learn every day. Are you here to enroll your child?"

"No. I've actually come for a job. I want to assist here."

She hesitates before she says, "I don't think I can pay you."

"You don't have to pay me. I love children. And I want to do something meaningful with my time, something other than shopping and taking care of the house. Believe me, the whole thing becomes a routine that threatens to drive you crazy after a few months."

"Well," she says. "Do you have a problem taking orders?"

"Not at all."

"From someone younger than you, I mean."

I stall on my answer, thinking, how old do I look to you? Wetin you dey feel like? You think say you still be omo? Let's cut the crap, woman. We're both in our forties.

"You see," she says, "Caesaria, my sister-in-law—I'm sure you met her on your way in—is the director. She takes care of the day-to-day running of the school. She handles the teachers. I'm just the proprietor, the supervisor."

"That won't be a problem."

"Okay, Mrs...?"

"Onyekachi Alakija. But call me Kachi." It's the third time I've told her my name.

"Okay, Kachi. I'll get back to you. May I have your number?"

"Sure."

We exchange numbers and I leave. When I don't hear from her, I call. I ask her to hear me out. And after I give her the speech of my life, she hires me.

THE TEACHING POSITION AT TENDERMINDS DAYCARE—I hear Caesarea came up with the name—isn't a swim in the lake. I've never changed diapers in my life, never had to wipe poop off a baby's butt. But I'm doing that now. Crap. I guess the daycare is a place of learning for me too. I get home late whenever it's my turn to oversee the collection of children. Those are the days I could use plenty of rest. The upside of working at the daycare is, I'm making friends. The mothers of Lekki Montana now have things to talk about with me. And my neighbors, the ones who were not so neighborly, now come to my house to chit-chat.

George and Jooji's kids have become play buddies, now that I've volunteered to do the picking up from school. George and I are doing much better too. He knows I hold the trump: get me upset and you won't be going to play with Jacob, Julian, and Jennifer. But even though our kids are closer, I can't say the same for Jooji and I.

There's hardly a month she doesn't travel out of the country with her husband John. I can understand the vacations in Dubai and Singapore, but I can't understand the three-day medical conference she had to attend with him in Beijing. She even travels with him when he has surgery to perform in some west African country. Call me paranoid, but I think she does it to avoid me. Whenever she's around to run the daycare, I look for any excuse to go to her office and speak with her. I like to compliment her. Oftentimes, I do it when she's least expecting it. Like when she's preparing to go out and checking her reflection in the mirror, or grinning at the end of a phone conversation, or making a face at a child, or when she's upset and talking to herself. Or miming a song and pretending she's on stage, thinking no one's around. I never pass up on the chance to tell her how good she looks. I think she thinks it's just flattery and I'm doing it because she's my boss (and I want her to start paying me), but I mean every word I say.

She happens to be the only person I know who still uses rollers to make her hair. I thought that culture died with blacks decades ago. But I love her short afro. It's not full and wavy as those of us who have bought into the western stereotype would have liked, still, it's equally impressive and would have made C.J. Walker proud—I'm talking about those short, sheeny black curls that leave no gaps in between, stiff and unbouncy in their ruffledness. If I could swap my Brazilian hair for a wig styled in her coiffure, I would do so in a flash.

I know when men see her, they see her slender frame, her height, and her erotic gait, thanks to her naturalesque Nicki Minaj rear end. But when I look at her, I see a woman with no fake hair, no fake lashes, no fake nails; I see a strong, confident woman stuck to her ways, as unimpressionable as a straw mat, a woman who reminds me of the allure of dames in the 80s. Jooji, na you biko. I wu ya, daa. Ezigbo nwata nwanyi.

ONE MORNING, while Tom and I are having an alfresco breakfast at our couples table like we usually do on Saturdays, Tom says, "Kachi, did you say anything to anyone, anything that would give them a reason to be concerned about you?"

I find his tone worrying. "No," I say.

"John called to inquire if you were getting any help, if you were seeing anyone. Now. Why would he ask me that?"

Tom watches me take in his words and say nothing. I'm doing my best not to let it show. Truth is, I'm white with shock.

How could Jooji do this to me? How could she betray me like this? I thought she was bigger than that. When I called to ask for the teaching job, I told her if I spent another month in the house I'd kill myself. At the time, George had gotten on my last nerve and I had come close to telling her I wanted to do things to him no mother should ever do to her child.

I held back only because I knew she wouldn't give me the job after that. What I'm trying to say is, I could have told her anything. I trusted her.

"Perhaps they were in the neighborhood and saw me going to the clinic. Maybe that's how they knew."

"I don't think John would have asked me if you were getting any help if they saw you there. Besides, you haven't been to see Dr. Wright in over a month. Don't think I don't know. Surely, you didn't think he wouldn't call me if you missed an appointment."

"I'm fine. You don't need to worry about me."

"I wasn't worried until now. Honestly, Kachi, I just wonder what you did to make the Jemedafes worried about you."

"I didn't do anything."

"Okay, okay. But they saw something. Perhaps you don't know what you did."

Tom returns to his phone. He likes to read the morning papers on his PDA. And he usually shares an article with me. But he's not doing that now. He's not drinking his coffee either. I bet it's turned cold from his dismissal of me. I know he'll leave me someday. I just know it.

My vital signs may still be intact, but I know my life is over. Everywhere I go I meet people who are concerned about me. When they ask how I'm doing, or how things are with me, I want to snap 'how do you mean?' Now that I know Jooji is just like them, there's no doubt in my mind my secret is out. I bet Caesaria knows. And who knows how many more. The next day, I resign from the daycare. Caesaria asks why and I say personal reasons. I won't confront Jooji just yet. I plan to do it with a gun. I search the house for the licensed gun Tom keeps for our protection. And when I can't find it, I ask him where it is.

"Why are you looking for it?" he retorts.

"Aren't you worried that it's lost?"

"It's not lost," he says.

"Then where is it?"

He doesn't reply.

"You don't know, do you? You just believe it will somehow show up someday, just like that. What if George found it? What do you think he would do with it? I know school shootings are quite common where he came from."

"Kachi, stop it. Stop your nonsense. For your information, shootings are common in America. America. Not Great Britain. And if you must know, I took away the gun."

"You did what?"

"I took away the gun." He doesn't raise his eyes to look at me.

"Oh, for the love of God, Tom, if I wanted to kill myself there are many ways I could do it."

To hell with him. This is just a minor setback in my plan. It's probably best I don't use a murder weapon they can trace back to me. Better to have someone pull the trigger. I wanted to do it myself so I could say to Jooji, "You think I'm crazy? I'll show you crazy," and then order her to take off her clothes and lie on the bed, make her strap one wrist to the bed frame with a curtain tie-back so I can do the same to the other wrist with little trouble from her. I'll stuff her panty down her throat until she can only make muffled noises, and then I'll strap her ankles to the bed with more curtain-tiebacks, and pull till she's spread-eagled on the bed. I'll then light a candle and pour hot wax on her bare flesh. I'll put some on her eyelids. On her neck. Her navel. Her cunt. I'll watch as she squirms and jerks her head up, reacting like she's never done for anything she's felt down there. I'll make her beg for mercy and I'll shout over her pleas, "It's only wax, bitch; it won't leave scars on your precious skin. Oh. Does it hurt? Good. Now you know how I feel."

Too bad I'll have to hire someone to do it for me. But what if I asked him to play her a recording of me before he blows her brains out? Yes. That's what I'll do. Even though she won't see my face, she'll hear the pain in my voice when I say, "I only wanted to be your friend, only wanted good things for you. But you've ruined that now. I thought you were better than this. Thought you were my friend. I trusted you. You don't know how it is for people like me because people like you don't have to try hard to fit in. Why should you? You're the darling of Lekki Montana. I wasn't doing too badly until you opened your mouth. I have my struggles just like everyone else. I have my secrets. I have fears too. I fear being alone. And I hate that I've had to live my life for others, had to live a life my mother chose for me. She said she would disown me if I ever came out. Living a false life and denying who you are can make you wish you were dead. Or in my case make you bipolar. Do you know how that is? Do you? I confided in you and what did you do? You betrayed me. So damn you to hell."

But how do I hire an assassin? I don't know the first thing about hiring them. Perhaps I should get a bodyguard and ask him to do a hit for me. Whatever I do, I must be careful whom I talk to. Better to be patient, Kachi. You don't want to engage anyone who isn't ready to die with your secret.

AFTER ABOUT A MONTH, our lives return to normal. Tom and I are good. I'm taking my meds again and I've gone to see my therapist three times in the last two weeks. I have better things to do than to dwell on Jooji (the COVID-19 pandemic is all over the news). She's not worth it. I hear she's a wreck after residents boycotted her daycare, just like that.

My phone rings. It's her name on the caller ID. Speak of the devil. I'm surprised to get a call from her. (She's never called me before.) 'Kachi, how could you?' is the first thing she says, not 'Kachi, how are you?' I can tell she's trying to stay calm.

"What did I ever do to you?" she says.

"I don't know what you're referring to. I'm afraid you've lost me."

"I know it was you."

"Me who did what?"

"Who told everyone John caught the Corona Virus while he was in China."

I hang up on her.

I didn't say that, and I can't be bothered with trying to convince her otherwise. She can believe what she likes—don't care what she thinks, stopped caring a long time ago. I never said John caught the virus. I simply said he was in China, not too far back. And I know for a fact he's been sick lately.

You're Becoming One of Those People

From the moment you stepped into the Lagos airport terminal and saw station agents standing with baggage carts, you knew something wasn't right. In any other airport, you could've just strolled over to the carts and picked one out. But here, they were all taken—by station agents. And they would charge you for what you could do for free (a consumer coup d'etat is what it is). You were so upset you had equated the choice of either paying for their service or battling with your luggage with having to choose between drinking from a puddle of mud or going thirsty.

Welcome to Lagos, you think sarcastically. Welcome to the land of the hustle, where we make life harder for others so we can profit, where one man's calamity is another man's opportunity; one man's mess, another man's scrambled eggs—and you mean this in the literal sense, like if several crates of eggs slipped from a truck and shattered on the road, one thing's for sure: some people will scoop them up and cook them.

The city always has someone somewhere waiting to capitalize on your bad situation. A street market around heavy traffic is an example:

the traffic forces motorists to drive slowly and this presents hawkers with valuable seconds to sell items like bottled water to passengers. A group of protesters reacting to a news story presents an opportunity. A shop on fire presents an opportunity. A committee set up by the government to investigate stolen public funds presents an opportunity. There are so many people here with nothing to do but wait for opportunities. And with the country already in a bad state, opportunity abounds, just ask our politicians. Sometimes you think, if all these people are so perceptive, why can't they come up with profit-making ideas of their own instead of festering around strategic spots, looking for people to hustle, like these station agents?

You manage to drag your luggage to the entrance, where more hustlers are waiting with visitors who are there to pick up familial or familiar faces or to pick up strangers they know by their names and phone numbers. You see your 5'5" elder sister in the crowd. She's craning her neck and waving to you. She looks different with her hair shorn (they called it 'the Anita Baker' back then, but it's a pixie cut today).

She asks the cart bandit to trundle your luggage to the gate, where you hope to charter a metro taxi as they are much cheaper than the taxis within the premises. He picks a fine time to tell you the parking lot is as far as he can go and pretends he had misunderstood your request, and even claims he would've informed you if you had been clear. This chap is sly. He's annoying. Well, lucky him: his overcharge you had foreseen; his under-performance you had not.

The city has tall stately buildings lining major highways. What you don't know is, they give the city a cosmetic façade by concealing the slums behind, places where the corporate world offers nothing but its back. You realize this when your taxi turns into a single lane that gets narrower and narrower as it takes you through squalid neighbourhoods with chaotic intersections and more chaotic intersections. Sad. It's like watching a beautiful woman take off her eyelashes, her eyebrows, her wig, her teeth, one eye...

Your disillusionment with your country started after you flunked med school. True, it was your fault, and you've accepted this as it is the unspoiled thing to do. And because when you think about it, who else was to blame for your not scoring higher in your first year, especially for not passing The Use of English, and the other second-semester English course, when English was your strongest subject? Who else was to blame for your ending up on probation in your first year and not knowing anything about it until it became official, a semester late? And this was the case because you were unconcerned, and you were unconcerned because you knew your grades wouldn't be good, and you really didn't want to know how bad. Who else was to blame for your not managing your allergies? And you had failed to manage your allergies because the doctors had misdiagnosed your condition; they had treated you for malaria, common cold, flu, or asthma, or—here comes your favorite—exam phobia. But then there was your single-parent mother, who had her issues and was more concerned with wrangling with the neighbors that she forgot to check up on your grades. And what about the school for graduating doctors without having them undergo an E.N.T. posting under the tutelage of a consultant like they have in other postings? (If the doctors had had a solid E.N.T. background, they would have known you had allergic rhinitis.) Or the government for not stopping the school's admissions board from admitting more students than its facilities could accommodate, all for more money. When you think about those over-shat toilets you were forced to use, and how you dreaded going into them, how your main focus shifted from your studies to getting through the week without shitting on yourself, you can't help but blame the authorities for not building hostels with toilets and shower rooms en suite.

You consider yourself a gentleman, and not just any gentleman, but an extreme one at that. Being an extreme gentleman means being prepared to go to great lengths to protect your mannerliness. (And you're not talking about pulling out chairs and opening doors; you're talking about giving respect and staying respectable.) You came to Lagos to honor your student-visa appointment with the U.S. Embassy. And if things go well, the international airport here will be your springboard to America, where you'll restart your medical program.

As the weeks to your day of reckoning before a US consular officer ticked away lento, you felt the city trying to erode your sense of self (your self-dignity, self-respect, self-composure, self-assuredness, self-determination—your good selves, basically) until you became one of those people. Suffice it to say, your first time in Lagos was one you'll never forget. It was more than a rude awakening; it was the beginning of an unmaking. Every so often, you had heard that popular Fela song 'I no be gentleman at all, I be African man, original' and had known it was you against them. While you were there, you experienced the streets from a commuter's point-of-view. That was as close as you got. The street gangs you saw were the bus touts, popularly called agberos. Still, you had a good glimpse of the city's bottom-feeders and their hustle.

One feature of the streets of Lagos is the molue. There's no other city street in the world where you'll find molues, those large buses that stick out in traffic, you simply can't miss their old-model design, their rusted, rundown appearance, or their cockeyedness as they career down the road, overburdened with passengers of three types: the sitting, the standing, and the hanging (and then there are the aspirants who run alongside them, bracing themselves to clamber into the aisle, or hang from the doors). These moving dumpsters make you wonder why anyone would choose to travel like this. Onlookers might not understand, but those who operate these rides and those who patronize them appreciate their common ground: extras: one party saves extra by getting on the cheapest mode of transport while the other makes extra by carrying twice the seating capacity. Your epiphany zeroes in on you, standing in the bus, and you see yourself for what you are: another cheapskate among cheapskates.

The molue lurches and teeters along the road and you plunge, yet again, into the large woman in front of you. Once, your face almost got caught between her breasts; another time, it got tangled up somewhere between the underside of her arm and her thighs. You're Mr. Ready With An Apology each time you crash into her. You're always sorry. You're sorrier for being there. You wonder how things could have gotten this bad, how public services could reach such dehumanizing standards. But mostly, you wonder about the woman: why she remains glued to you even after someone gets off the bus, giving standers like you more elbow room. It makes you want to scream, "What's the problem, Orobo? Too heavy to shift?" You want to say something but stay silent. Your silence comes from believing you're not there, from not wanting to involve yourself in a scene you couldn't be a part of. You may have caught others like you, mute and trying to be invisible. They may have glanced at you as they hung from the handrails, ears plugged with headphones, heads bobbing to the soundtracks of their stark realities.

In another embarrassing episode you had on a bus, you were running late for your USAID student-orientation class and decided to take a danfo (they're smaller, with black and yellow stripes). You were in a big hurry so you had climbed into the only seat left: the seat between the driver and the front passenger. The seat was not factory-fitted. It, just like you, was not supposed to be there. You had sat with the gearbox between your legs like a giant dildo, and all through the ride, the driver had stepped on the clutch and reached for your crotch, in the figurative sense.

You once left a tin of Milo open by accident and discovered your mistake two days later. By then, the city's humid coastal weather had turned the powdered beverage into a hard crumb. You wonder if the same thing can happen to people in this city. You're talking about blue-bloods turning into boors. It would probably take two years, not two days like in the tin of Milo. Your theory about people hardening in the city piques your curiosity and you begin to see those around you as individuals in different stages of mental decline. When frustrations get the better of them, they become angrier and more brazen. It's all part of coping with Stress and the City. And so, you took a closer look at your sister, your brother, and Big C, all of whom had lived longer in the city.

Your sister had seemed edgier than you recalled. She had a knack for complaining about the littlest things: Who left dirty dishes in the sink? Who left the toilet seat up? How many times do I have to tell you to return the magazines to the bookrack when you're done? Who sat on my bed and forgot to straighten the covers? Your brother, on the other hand, didn't seem like he'd changed much. He still imploded like he used to. Typically, he goes into shutdown mode each time something upsets him. He seems to brood more, these days. You're not a psychologist, but you think he protects his sanity by brooding. Big C returns late from work, most times. Rather than spend hours in rush-hour traffic, after closing from his bank job, your cousin goes to the gym or his taekwondo club. You imagine it's there he lets out steam. Heeyah!

Out in the streets, it's not unusual to run into pedestrians talking to themselves, sounding fey, not caring who's listening, some angry, some not. You came up with a name for it: Lagos City Loquacity, the descent into madness. As a closet writer, you often carry a scrapbook with you so you can write down things that pop into your head, things you want to save for later. Unfortunately for you, the day you came up with Lagos City Loquacity, you didn't have your scrapbook. You were in a danfo, beside a woman trying to make her baby stop crying.

SHE HUGS IT, shakes it, pats it on the back, throws it in the air and catches it. She does all you can think of, but give it the titty. Can't she see it? The child is hungry and all she does is blather at it. You've never heard such absurd baby-talk. She's adding to the noise and driving you crazy. Before you know it, you're speaking out your thoughts and shouting over the noise: Lagos City Loquacity! Lagos City Loquacity! You're practically chanting it now. Lagos City Loquacity. For fuck sake give it the titty! For fuck sake give it the titty! You raise your voice when the noise gets louder and forget to lower it when it stops. Uh-oh. The passengers are turning to stare at you. Shit. Shit-shit-shit, shit. The look in their eyes says it all.

Weekends in Lagos were always fun. Street parties were everywhere. It was at times like those that you had seen the glamor of the city, the humor too.

TGIF. You're on your way to a vaudeville in the Muson Centre called 'A Nite of a Thousand Laffs', all four of you (Big C is treating). After the show, you head back to the car, to Big C's Honda parked on the side of the road. A small group of guys heckles you along the way. They speak as though you owe them money. You don't remember asking anyone to watch the car. Are they parking attendants? Big C warns the three of you to keep your mouth shut. Just keep moving, he says, if they can't get money, they'll be happy with a fight. That's when you see it in their eyes: how much they hate you. They think those better-off than them are mean for not helping out. Area boys, that's who they are. They insult you. They taunt you. They get in your face. They do everything but touch you. They want you to touch them first, or say something back, but you ignore them and get in the car. They're still yelling as you drive off. What babies, what losers!

Some weekends you had an event to attend. Sometimes it was a wedding, other times it was a graduation ceremony like the time you had gone with your brother to Akoka to attend his old classmate's graduation:

After the ceremonies, several family-hosted picnics commence at the convocation ground, just outside the university's main auditorium. Without warning, hordes of uninvited guests arrive and mingle with the crowd. They grab plates and line up at food collection points. Animals. Mongrels. Area boys! Shoo. Go on, get lost. Scores keep coming. It's hard to tell them apart so there's little the hosts can do but ask them nicely to get lost—forget it, you can't abash them into leaving if you tried—and when that doesn't work, they stop the servers from dishing out more food. But if they think they've ruined their fun, they can think again: the area boys photo-bomb the group photos; they flank your brother's old classmate and his family and unsettle them with their smiles.

Another time you had your outing disrupted you were at the beach. An old busker came up to you and began to play.

HE SMILES AS HE STRUMS HIS GUITAR, but you're not fooled. He's an area boy. Politely, you say 'no thanks', even though you would much rather have said 'get the fuck away', and maybe you should have because he sings himself hoarse and gets all red-eyed when you refuse to tip him. Bloody beggars. If you gave him money, he'd still be poor, and still be acting like it's all your fault. Fuck him. Weary from his rants, he just stands there, staring. He stares and stares. You can literarily feel the weight of his hate bearing down on you. But so what? You don't care, as long as he's quiet. A good thing he's carrying a guitar, not a gun.

YOU'RE IN A CYBERCAFE filling out your visa application when a guy you know from your street pops his head over your privacy panel and says hi. He asks what you're doing and you tell him you're filling your SEVIS form. He asks what that is, and you explain. He says he doesn't blame you for wanting to leave the country, some people think it's cowardly, but he thinks they're fools, certainly not lovers of knowledge, or people who want to be the best at what they do, because people like that are ready to go anywhere. You guys talk about all the things that are wrong with the country, contrasting her with America, the America you know from watching the news and listening to rap music. He says the reason why the system works in America is because America tries to identify gifted people. That's why many go from rags to riches over there, he says, not like here where you have to know someone or have to bribe someone. He says he's a rapper looking for a record deal and that 'Arrested Development' would have been his artiste name if an American rap group hadn't thought of it first. He says he's known as 'Hip-hop Pauper' in the underground. And you say, Nice. You think he said 'Poppa', 'Hip-hop

Poppa', so you tell him you like it because it makes him sound like an overlord. You're a writer, you say, you write fiction and nonfiction. You tried the spoken word, once, but it's not for you, you say, you're not the showbiz type. Just look at you guys, he says. Talents wasting, he says. All people do in this country is complain, complain, complain, and just run their mouths. No one does a fucking thing, he says. You can't agree more. Fucking noise makers, you say. You guys say fuck this and fuck that, fuck them all, and experience a sense of camaraderie that comes with saying the word 'fuck', and not giving a fuck.

You ask him what he's doing at the café and he says internet-scamming. Actually, he didn't say 'scamming' (or 'internet'); he used the local term 'yahoo-yahoo' and gave you a wink. It's what many young people are into. He talks about how he's forced to do what he does because the whole shit-hole system doesn't work. You tell him there's no need for him to explain, you understand. You shake hands, snap fingers, and sign peace before you part ways. You go back to your form-filling and he goes back to searching for mugus online. That's how it is, how it ought to be. They do their thing; you do yours. Nope. You won't get on the high horse and judge those swindlers. To scam a few, they have to spam so many, and that takes hard work.

You remember the time you were watching The Good Times with your brother when a news story broke and the station interrupted regular programming to make a public announcement.

THERE'S A BODY IN THE STREETS and the station is calling on the local authorities to take care of it. The report doesn't say who died because he or she is, as of yet, unidentified, some poor bastard no one will miss, likely. Like a tramp or a madman. Finding a body in the street is no biggie, your brother says, it happens all the time. He says it's a matter for the police when it's a murder or a hit-and-run; a matter for the sanitary workers when the body looks thin and starved, and those are the ones that usually get announced like this. He says he once saw a body in Mile Two and people just walked around it like it was a dead dog; no one raised a finger or an eyebrow. But why are you surprised? Without social services, that's what things will come to. The city is sick and everyone knows it. In medical parlance, when it's chronic, the city endures; when it's acute, it simply waits for a crisis to deal with it. Well, so much for ho-hum affairs. The Good Times resumes and you go back to watching. Jimmie Walker is hilarious, he's dyn-o-mite! You bet living in a Yankee ghetto beats living anywhere in this city.

On the day of your interview, you had reached the US embassy well ahead of time. Outside the embassy gates, you saw a crowd of protesters. Well, they looked like protesters, but you soon learned they were visa applicants, just like you.

You ask a well-dressed man watching the scene what the problem is, and he says they won't let them in. He says he's been coming for weeks and they won't even listen to him.

"Why won't they?" you ask him.

"Do I know for them? These people have issues."

"Did you show them your appointment letter?"

"You, have you shown them yours?' he snaps at you.

It's your cue to scram. You sense his aggression and back away. You know what's going on here. These people have no appointments yet they have the gall to speak with indignation. You overhear one of them telling a gateman that he has an inquiry to make that none of them can answer or bring back an answer to, no one but an embassy official. And something in that utterance flicks a light switch in your brain.

Area boys. That's who they are.

It's all in the fibbing, the pack mentality, the blustering despite low self-esteem, the cry-baby wrangles, and the list goes on. Something in their aplomb, that cocksureness of brazened paranoiacs, of scrappy idlers, incenses you to the point it makes you want to act out your rage—and get off from it, from beating them off with whips, shouting, "Get away from me, mangy mongrels." You've run into them a couple of times, enough times to know their hustle. They're everything you never want to be and the very thing that if you became, would make you not want to look in another mirror for fear you might recognize the gilded guttersnipe.

You didn't expect to find them here, didn't think they had the same aspirations as you, and this worries you because, frankly, they're not that different from you. In appearance, you mean. It's not obvious, at a glance, that they're bullies who take their bad behaviors to the haunts of the rich, pestering opportunists at best, pickpockets and petty thieves at worst. And it's not as if an interview will give them away or make them act up in public.

Broken Sleep

Twelfth moon of the long aftermath. We are many miles from Cyangugu, the rubble that once was home. Life is humble. We walk several miles during the day and rest in the evening. I look forward to our bonfire carnivals when we gather around the largest fires ever made and sing ourselves hoarse. We sing to fan the flames in our hearts, sometimes we dance. Anything to remind us of our roots in these strange parts.

At bedtime, the little children keep us up. They have nightmares. Their nonstop outbursts make my spine stiffen. Many are orphans. Instead of having their mothers embrace them, they have strangers to shake them. "Wake up," they say. "You are safe now. The worst is over." And I wonder how they know that for sure. I still see images in my sleep, memories I am trying to forget. They make me want to run and run and just keep running. But when I open my eyes, they are gone. Gone are the men engulfed in flames, screaming and scrambling about before sinking to their knees, and crashing headlong to the ground. Gone are girls my age and younger, wriggling in the hands of men who ride them until they are still (or snap their necks to make them still). Gone is the inside of the cathedral where my big sister, carrying her two-month-old baby, scrambles up to the choir loft and sits on the railing thirty meters up. She will turn her back to us and slump backward and fall, clutching her baby in her arms. And gone are the soldiers ordering us to pick up the chopped-off heads of our fathers and uncles and kick them towards them like footballs. When I do see something, it is not like before. It is like a reflection in a lake, nothing more. If I sweep my hand across the surface, I can make it go away.

We are on our way to the French-protected camps at Goma and have just passed Gisenyi. I hear there is a white doctor there. They say he has medicine for people who cannot sleep. I hear there is good food too. Ndika says the white man has beautiful cities with buildings that tower over streets, taller than the tallest mountains. They have no wars because there is plenty of food for everyone. They have so much food that the bad, greedy ones grow fat and fat until they burst and die.

It is midday. We have stopped to rest under a cool shade not far from the Virunga Mountains. I see Volcan Karisimbi wearing white clouds like a chief's hat. A strong ray of sun strikes it from behind with a ring that glints in certain parts, outlining its topmost edges. For now, it glows slate blue, a deeper blue than the sky. Ndika goes on and on about all the food he misses and his plans to join his elder brother in America. Ndika is short for Ndikatubane, which means let us live together. He is part Burundian, part Rwandan.

"They will take us to France," I say. "America is not fighting this war. There is no oil in Rwanda, that is why. That is what everybody is saying."

He looks at me with wide eyes, as if I have just kicked him in the teeth. "So you can talk? You used to just listen."

I nod.

"They will take you and the others to France, but I will be going to America because I have a brother there and you do not. That is how they do." He stresses the 'you do not'.

Ndika is restless. He says he needs to empty his bowels. He wants me to go with him across the open field to the large rocks on the other side, less than a mile away, so he can do it behind them. He wants me to go with him so I can stand guard. We make our way through the grassy plains, heading for the rocks at the base of the Virunga, moving further and further away from our tree shelter, and our tribe.

"Ndika, Azizi, where are you two going?" Souza calls after us.

I tell him. I have to shout so he can hear me. Ndika hisses and lowers his eyes. He is not happy with my saying the truth. Or maybe it was the way I put it—I said he wants to go and take a big poop. He is especially not happy that Imana is there to hear it. He likes Imana but does not know how to tell her. He is always shy around her. Even after what we saw last night, he still likes her.

Imana and the other youngsters stop picking leaves for soup and stare at me. They are squinting as if I have just thrown sand in their eyes.

Souza is surprised too. "Oh, so you talk now?" he says. "The only thing you said before was your name."

I nod.

"Well, don't go too far," Souza says. "There are savage dogs about. And they like young boys like you."

"The mbwa mwitu?" Ndika asks.

"No, not the African wild dog but the pets you left at home. What is the name of your dog?"

"Tiger."

Souza laughs a big, hearty laugh, his hands at his hips. He recovers and fixes the machine gun slung over his shoulder. "Well, if you see Tiger again, run for your life," he says. "I am sure he now hunts with a pack and he eats abandoned little boys to survive."

Souza is eighteen, three years our senior. He is a soldier, a runaway. He joined our party a few days back. The Tutsi militia he fled could be looking for him and heading our way, and if they find him, they will find us too. Ndika thinks he is bad news. He did not think that when he first arrived, only after last night.

LAST NIGHT, while everyone was partying at the bonfire carnival, we chanced on Souza and Imana in a dark spot. They were naked, naked like in newborns. She was clinging to him like a little monkey on her mother's belly, thighs spread apart and legs folded over his arms, knees raised almost as high as his shoulder, feet flexed and pointy. Something spoke to me as we watched them, watched Souza slam into her repeatedly, his grunts, her moans, his grunts, her moans, the moon carving out their bodies. There were pleasures in this world I was yet to discover. I had seen the bitter, not so much the sweet. I had not wanted to start speaking yet until I saw Ndika's eyes and nose running. His prize had been contaminated. Imana was making a baby with Souza. And the chances were, they will marry. If I had spoken then, I would have said to my friend, "Pain is part of life, pleasure too. If you do not let one renew you, the other will become you."

WE TRAVEL WITH SCOUTS. They walk ahead of the tribe. If we are ambushed, we will hear their screams and retreat, and their sacrifice would have saved the tribe. This morning I feel differently about scouts. I do not want to look at them that way anymore. Big Chief has put Ndika and me in a team of scouts. Scouts are the real leaders; they choose the path their tribesmen follow. We stay in sight and wave to them from miles. 'The coast is clear,' we sign. 'Come, come.'

It is lunchtime. While some of us eat, others are playing close to the old bridge we discovered not long ago. We have scoured its near edge for danger and found nothing, but because of the jungle below it, Souza and Big Chief have decided that the rest of the tribe should camp a safe distance from it. The bridge is wooden and rickety, creepy. It creaks as if a ghost were walking across it. It is wide enough for one motor car at a time, but I am not sure any driver will even dare. Tree branches reach over it from both sides. They are not leafy enough to give it shade and so we can see most of its length. Parts of it are black with mould that remind me of the loaf of bread I had to throw away. It does not look safe. Some boards are missing. More gaps in the wood appear mainly towards the other end. "We will cross in groups of six," Big Chief says. Luckily, there are no very- old people travelling with us. It is the fat ones I worry about, like Auntie Felicia, who used to own a provision store in my part of Cyangugu. She is the only person in the tribe who is not a total stranger.

The jungle below-deck is dense. Tree leaves sway in the wind. They make a fizzy sound like the sound Sprite makes when you pour it into a cup. From where the bridge starts, the land slopes down sharply and you cannot see the bottom because of the umbrellas of leaves block-ing it. Instead of a river, the lowland has leafy trees growing from it. Souza says it is a rift valley. "This one is very fertile, so fertile varieties of plants are growing on it," he says. It looks deep, deep enough to keep tall trees below the surface. From the middle of the bridge, you can reach out and touch the leaves of giant trees. It is dark and frightening under the bridge. And that is good for our game of hide-and-seek. Our play quickly turns into a game of dare: Who has the nerve to go the farthest in Trench-land?

We form teams of two: Ndika and I, Paul and Koroma, Junior and Samuel. Together, we pick our way through thick bushes. I am careful, but I am scared, mostly. It is not so dark after your eyes have adjusted to the light pouring in through the gaps in the tree shades. In fact, it is not dark at all. There is wild banana. And oil palm. And plenty of grass growing in between. The deeper we go, the steeper the valley gets. We pluck acacia fruit pods as we slide down.

After we have gone a good distance, Ndika says, "Azizi, stop. Let's not go any further. It will be too hard to climb back up if we do."

He might be right. We have just jumped down a small cliff; getting back up will take some effort. But I don't think the land to our left is cliffy, judging from the slant of the thickets covering it. Something is strange, though.

"Do you hear that?" I say to Ndika. "What?"

"The noise of the others. It has stopped." Before now, I could tell who was ahead from the rustling of leaves around us. But now the rustles have stopped.

"They've gone back up. We've won. Yay. Scared babies. Come on. Let's mark this spot so we can prove we came this far."

"After that, then we go?"

Ndika laughs at my expression. It is relaxing. "Yes. After that, we go back up," he says.

We look around for a marker to anchor to the ground, and as we do, Ndika calls my name. "Look at this," he says, holding up a boot he picked from behind the gorse at the bottom of a small cliff. It's a soldier's boot. It doesn't look old.

"I'm keeping it," he says.

"Sssh," I say with a finger to my lips. "Someone is here."

Ndika's eyes widen and return to size. "It's not going to work," he says. "You can't scare me."

I move away from the cliff and crouch down behind some tall grasses. I beckon him to do the same. He obeys. We stay crouched and silent. Minutes pass. Nothing happens. Suddenly, we hear sniffles and a muffled cry. The sound neither approaches nor wanes. Whoever- it- is is hiding somewhere nearby. Listening out for us, perhaps. If one of the others is planning to jump out from the bushes and surprise us, then why is he crying? We wait. Whoever-it-is waits too. He wants us to move first, and we want him to move first, and so no-one does anything. More minutes pass. Ndika fidgets. I warn him not to get up. My whisper is raspy and breathy. I hear boots—I think a soldier is approaching. It is too close for comfort. I can hear a conversation. I can't hear it clearly because it is low and panty. My heart is beating fast, trying to thump out of my chest. My ears are alert to any disturbance around me. I hear Ndika crying. Shrubs shield his face from my view.

We remain flat on our bellies. The men are speaking in low growls now. They are telling someone to be quiet or else they will shoot him dead. If he shouts, they will shoot. If he runs, they will shoot. Soldiers. They have captured the others and they are looking for us. I wish I could turn into a snake and slither away unnoticed. The men move off and everywhere becomes silent again, just the fizzing of trees. I know they are not far. They have probably picked a different spot to listen out for us. Ndika is breathing hard. He keeps making the pig grunts of someone sucking back his mucus. When he cries, he always has catarrh. Strong winds swirl around us and fade. I hear footsteps. Panting.

Bushes shifting. Lots of shifting. Someone is running. "Stop," a man says in Hutu. It's a chase. People are running… downhill. Someone howls. They have caught him because I can hear him pleading. They are beating him. "What did I tell you?" they say. "Did you not hear me say you should stop? "They call him a cockroach, a disgusting thing on the face of the earth. They kick and slap him. He cries. Others are crying with him. Their sniffles grow into wails. There is a gurgling sound. The soldiers are choking the runner. They warn those crying to stop and they obey. The gurgles of the strangled peter out like a tap that hisses as you close it. Silence. They move off again. I am sure they have left a body somewhere. But whose? Paul's? Junior's? Koroma's? Or Samuel's? We remain in our positions long after they are gone. Finally, I crawl over to Ndika and slump down beside him.

"We have to go warn the others," I say. He nods.

"Bastards. They were here waiting for us all the time."

My thoughts are broken when I hear someone call my name. He calls Ndika's name too. And Paul's. And Junior's. It's Souza. He is asking us to come out, to stop playing, and get ready to cross the bridge.

One of the scouts calls out to him. It sounds like Paul. He says he has sprained an ankle. He needs some help. "Where are you?" Souza shouts. "Down here," he responds. Yes, it is Paul. But there is shakiness in his voice. I know he is not wounded. The soldiers are making him say he is so they can draw Souza in.

Somewhere at the top of the valley, Souza inches down. I hear him. He is carrying his machine gun, I imagine. He never goes far without it. Someone is crying. One of the other scouts, I suppose. He knows what will happen. They will kill Souza. After that, they will kill him too. They will kill us all unless someone alerts the tribe to them, the murderous men hiding in the trenched jungle. Souza continues to descend. "I'm coming," he says. "Paul, where are you?"

"Souza, it's a trap. Don't come! They want to kill you." Those are my words but Ndika beat me to it. Where is he? It is getting dark, too dark to see.

Shots are fired. I hear feet scuffling back up. More shots. I get up and run. I run downhill. I fall on my belly and roll on my side. I let my body slide down until a thicket catches me. The shooting stops. I lie flat on my back and slowly raise my head to look up. Everywhere is dark. Someone shouts a command, and several others begin to shriek. They stampede up the valley. Hundreds of soldier boots. Guns ring out and bombs explode. Flashes of light crackle over tree branches. The sound of missile launches plays a tune with the rat-tat-tat of smaller firearms. The tribe is scream-ing. People are running scared. There is lots of squealing, battle cries, and others I don't want to imagine. I am crying. The uproar reminds me of the night jackals raided our chicken house. Still, the ambush had not gone as planned, thanks to Ndika. Where is he? With the stealth of a jungle cat, I claw my way back up to search for him. I find him sprawled on the ground, face down, too scared to move. I edge closer. The longer we stay here, the likelier a soldier will find us. We have no guns so we must flee, sink deep into the plains of the valley, and hide there.

I grab him by the shoulder and give him a hard shake. "Ndika, let's go."

He does not move. I try to pull him up. He is stiff, stiff like a full bag of rice. Around his head is a goop of red, a small puddle. Something is oozing from his right temple. I don't wait, my legs carry me off. I run as if I have just seen a ghost. I run, run and run. I have to get away from there. I want to get away from everywhere. I don't want to die. I want to marry and make babies. I want lots of babies. In the white man's country. I reach the plain of the valley and crouch under the leaves of a young banana plant.

The shelling reduces to rhythmic gunshots. The soldiers are celebrating, shooting in the air, from the sound of it. They are singing. And I believe... dancing. A harvest dance, I imagine. I push away banana leaves and peer up the valley. The acacia on the slope rustle, and it is not the wind making them. It can't be soldiers either because I can smell fear behind them. Some of those who escaped the raid have found their way into the valley. Their heads poke out from the leaves as they gaze up the hill. They seem to be thinking of going back up when the coast is clear. They can't. They will be killed.

"Psst," I call to three heads. They look back. Slowly, I stand up from behind my banana plant so they can all see me, their scout, and see that I'm brave. I beckon them down. Come with me, I sign. Slowly, they emerge from their hiding spots. They are more than I first counted. They are seven or so. Most of them are children but there are two women among them. Carefully, quietly, they slip down to the base of the valley and gather around me.

"We can't go back up," I say. "We must go this way." I point into the jaws of an even darker, less welcoming territory, where all the giant trees are rooted. "They don't know we are here. If they knew they would come after us. So relax."

They nod, choosing not to say a word. Some are not sure they are awake. I know that feeling.

They wait for me to move first and they follow. I creep between thick trunks of massive trees, trying to move in a straight line. I tread as lightly and silently as I can. I think of the old wooden bridge, trying to recall how long it had looked. By my calculation, we will not have far to go before the ground starts sloping upwards again towards the other side. Something smells. Smells like food burning. I follow the scent, veering away from my course. I follow it all the way to a campsite, a deserted campsite. A soldiers' camp. And it seems like they left in a hurry. There are boots, pots, shaving sticks, blankets, tins of water, clothes rolled into bundles, and jerry cans. I open one of the jerry cans and check its content. Just as I thought. It is petrol. For setting roaches like us ablaze. The place is empty. But soon the soldiers will come back for their things. They will look for petrol to use in burning those they have captured.

"Quick, grab all the jerry cans you can find," I say to the others, handling two tall cans.

The group listens without questioning. It is as if they know too. Climbing up the valley will be harder now, but it is worth it. When we get to the top, we will pour out all the petrol into the valley, and start a forest fire, and hope it burns all their things together with the old bridge.

Signs

I lower my head to my knees to pray when I feel the plane's tyres leave the tarmac. The passenger in the seat across the aisle watches me with fascination. He sees me staring back and smiles sheepishly. He's a foreigner, European, I think. Not that I care, but he probably thinks me primitive: a believer in the inexplicable and a questioner of the explicable. In a sense, he's right. But, hey, there's more to it. I believe the inexplicable in our lives are like whispers from God, they try to tell us something. Ignore them at your own peril.

The cabin slants. Up and up. It's almost vertical now. I fix my gaze on the cockpit door, now a steep climb away—I'll need to cling to headrests and pull myself up to get to the pilot and give him a good slap to snap out of it. As I rollercoaster upwards, preparing for a loop in the air, I limn my backrest like a dielectric: head straight, spine erect, eyes shut. But, thankfully, the plane dips forward and, steadily, the cabin levels off.

I broke a vow by getting on this plane. After the Bellview and Sosoliso air crashes of 2005, which were months apart, I had sworn never again to fly if I could take the bus instead. Blame it on my push to begin a new chapter in my life, like a mindless charge across the Serengeti. My life is finally taking off, so why not take a plane. I'll be getting married soon. My bride will be flying in from Sydney. But before she arrives, I have schedules to meet, places to be, people to see, and ceremonies to perform.

My decision never to fly again came while discussing the allegations that the Federal Aviation Authority accepted bribes to overlook some safety standards flouted by airlines. An old friend whom I ran into at an airport said that one of those standards was making sure that all old aircraft were phased out. He said that you could always tell an old plane from a new one from the way they gained altitude. If they muscled their way up, then, they were old. Muscling their way up meant hoisting and weaving to their sides, giving you a hang glider's view of the ground below. But isn't that how they all climb? I had asked, appalled. My friend simply laughed. That's when I realized I had never been on a new plane before. And with this came Survivor's Gratitude.

Messiah! So I could have been one of those crash victims who have bodiless graves because their bodies were never found. And their bodies were never found because they were incinerated, obliterated, burnt to ashes, cremated upon impact, and scattered for the wind to own. Armed with this knowledge, which came almost by accident, I realized that if I ever found myself in a plane that rose in the air by tilting sideways and dipping on its wings, I would most certainly have visions of screeching winds ripping the plane apart before lighting it up like a piece of straw between rocks, and would most certainly die of a heart attack before the fatal plummet. And so I didn't do planes anymore.

My heart lands with a bump-bump (front and back tires) and taxis down the runway. I see the world differently now, a spate of wisdom swamping me and freeing me from everything it's ever learned, everything it was ever taught, allowing me to make sense of things I never questioned and didn't realize were questionable, like why Americans call the scoring play in their brand of football 'a touchdown', not something stupid like 'goal'.

I relax my brace position, mumble a thank-you prayer, and open my eyes again. I see passengers standing in line, waiting for the plane door to open. I'm in the way of two of them—the passengers in the middle and the window seats of my row want to pass. I quickly make room for them and they island me on my seat, leaving me with a clear view of the window on our row. The window is unshuttered, and through it, I can see a crystal polygon gleaming silvery opaque in the sun.

I move a seat closer for a better view. The control tower shoots up on one side of the terminal. It's a steeple wide enough to fit offices. Little buses scoot towards the plane and even littler people sprinkle out of them. I feel like I'm in a quadruple-decker bus.

OUTSIDE THE PLANE, I strap on my knapsack and sling my coat over one arm. I take a cab to First Artillery, to the Catholic Institute of West Africa (CIWA), where Nyekachi said he was staying.

After nearly an hour of holdups made worse by bad roads and traffic diversions, I reach the entrance of the church, which looks like a small tollgate. The large signboard on one side of the gate says 'Our Lady of the Holy Rosary Chaplaincy Catholic Institute of West Africa (CIWA)'. I call Nyekachi on my cell phone and he tells me where to find him. The gateman directs us. We drive into the institute's manicured premises. There is a church building and a grotto on our left, and what looks like an outdoor shrine on the right. It has a star-shaped roof. It's flat and it slants outwards in an aerodynamically impressive way. We pass the church and head towards the campusier parts of the institute.

The place is serene, almost heavenly. I recall what Nyekachi said came to his mind when he first came here, a Jesuit regent: If this is poverty, I can't wait to see chastity. I had smiled then, but I'm not smiling now, now that it's public knowledge that he had impregnated a girl while he was here, a girl who came forward after his ordination. (He says he did not break his vow of celibacy, as defined by the church, since he is still unmarried. The only thing he broke was his obligation of continence, which is not a vow. All I know is, technically, he must still be a priest since they haven't thrown him out.)

WE ARE SITTING ON A BENCH sculpted from concrete, Nyekachi and I, facing a trunk road within the institute. The road is empty—nothing but lizards run over it, chasing, stopping, starting and stopping again, their heads bobbing up and down in little lizard pants. I am pressing down on my knapsack with one side of my body, sunglasses on, hands interlocked over my chest. Nyekachi asks me how long I've known her. I say three weeks. He wants to know what time I'd like for us to leave tomorrow, and I say before ten.

He says one woman brought sin into the world, and another, salvation. He stops mid-sentence and gives me a vacant stare. "I'm not saying my son is sin," he says, "but you know what I mean, Chizoba." I do. He is not contrasting Eve with the mother of Jesus, as one might think; he is contrasting the mother of his child with the woman I plan to marry. I'm guessing sin means being barred from saying mass publicly, and salvation means turning the family fortunes around, which he believes I'm about to do. I wonder why it never occurred to me how similar our motives were for choosing the different paths we chose. Yes, I've always known my rascally, now-reformed elder brother and I feel the same way about the country, but I'm just now appreciating how these feelings help form our major decisions in life.

A siren peals. Power is back. Blackouts are part of our daily lives. They can last up to nine hours. Even more. The sirens are important because they alert us to the precious minutes we have to do our ironing, charge our phone batteries, turn on the water pump, watch television (things like this) before the power goes off. The blare of a siren doesn't just tell us power is back, it tells us to get up and get on with our lives. Without them, we could languish in darkness and miss out on our window of opportunity. I think of them as a metaphor for something, something personal in our lives. I guess they're signs too.

Nyekachi sees me checking my phone and says, "May I see her?" I hand him my phone with my bride's photograph on the home screen. He looks at it, stays on it for a while, and hands it back to me. He slouches forward on the bench, his forearms resting on his laps, hands dangling between his thighs. His eyes are fixed somewhere between his feet, zombie-like. He lifts his head and sees me watching, waiting for him to say something, and sighs.

"This is so not you," he says. Of course, it's not. It's her. "You're so…" He racks his brain for the word. "Provincial," he says. "Disciplined," he says again. I don't know if he's adding or changing his mind. "This is the most… way-out thing you've ever done," he says. "You're the one who should have been the priest."

"So what do you think?" I ask.

"She looks fresh, affluent fresh. If her freshness masks her age, it's called formaldehyde fresh." He laughs. "But she's affluent fresh, she is. How old is she?"

"Twenty-eight."

He laughs again. It's a short you've-been-had sort of laugh.

"Chizoba," he says, shaking his head. "She's is in her late thirties. But forget it. It doesn't matter."

No, it doesn't. But she's not in her late thirties. She doesn't that swollenness that comes with advancing age, but she's just plump. She's shiny-fair, jowly-chinned, and beady-nosed. She has high cheekbones and a short tilapia mouth, lips like two flattened petals, indelicately luscious, good for kissing in upward and downward strokes. In almost every picture I've seen of her, her brows are always drawn with an eyebrow pencil. And in one, where she's wearing heavy makeup, she looks Oriental, like a geisha. She's a little too flat-faced for me, but that's okay. What I admire most about her, besides her lips, is the sheen in her complexion, the smoothness of her round face, and the glow in her slightly deep-set eyes.

"What's her name?" "Ijeoma."

There isn't much else to say. He knows how we met (we met on the internet), knows why I've come to him, and seems to know why I'm marrying her. I hand him his traditional attire—we'll be wearing matching clothes—and we say goodbye. I take a taxi to Elelenwo, where our parents live.

Father is sick. He's been battling partial stroke coupled with diabetes for years now. Hopefully, he'll hang on until I can fly him abroad for proper treatment.

Father is on the front porch when I arrive. He is hunched over a meal that heat fumes are rising from. It's something yellow and starchy that looks like eba, and so happens to be …eba. Who heaped his plate with gummy, gelatinous scoops shaped like the bowl they came from? Carbs. The man is slowly killing himself.

"Good afternoon, Papa."

"Inginia. You don come? Carry chair siddon make we chop," he says, unable to turn his neck to look at me.

I sink into the chair opposite his. "Papa, you shouldn't eat this quantity of food, you know that. What you need most is vegetable and meat."

"Wetin I go do, kwanu? You no chop, you die; you chop, you die." I raise his bowl and tip it slightly to one side. I swirl the soup around to expose chunks of meat, but all I see are sops of eba. The soup is parsimonious in vegetable. Its aroma doesn't rise and wrap around you. "Is there meat in this thing?" I ask. "Papa, have you eaten it?"

"No."

I hold the steaming bowl in my face, ashamed to look up. When was the last time I sent him money? How did I think he got by on his pension? In this biting economy, you have to be rich to support your aged parents the way you ought to.

Papa calls me 'Inginia' because I studied waste-management engineering, but what he doesn't know is that I'm a cross between an engineer and a waste-disposal man, and since the country won't invest in waste-management technology—in recycling machines and sewage systems—that leaves me a waste-disposal man. I like to think of myself as an environmental engineer. It's not totally untrue: I've been roaming the environment, engineering my curriculum vitae to land a job.

LATE-MORNING THE NEXT DAY, Ezeugo, meets up with us at the bus park in Water Lines. He's my best friend and will be my best man. He's from Abia and so he has a better understanding of Owerri (the dialect of Igbo spoken by my bride's family) than my brother and me, who are Ikwerre. Marriage introductions are cultural exchanges between families. They go smoother when the two families share a common native language.

"Chizzy," Ezeugo says. "Did you bring schnapps?"

"No," I say.

"What will we present?"

"Ourselves."

Nyekachi smiles.

"Don't worry," Ezeugo says. "When we get to Owerri, I will take you to a wine shop where you can choose from the finest wines. Mba nu, we can't go empty-handed."

"True," Nyekachi agrees.

Ezeugo turns to Nyekachi. "Father Nyekachi. Remember, while you are on this mission, you are not representing Christ; you are representing your father, your earthly father. So you need to represent. You know what I mean, don't you?"

Ezeugo likes to slip in a question at the end of his sentences. He does it for effect. I think he thinks it's the way big men talk. He thinks of himself as a paralegal at a law firm in Old GRA, but he's a barrister's errand boy. He has a diploma in marketing, but it doesn't stop him from parading himself as a lawyer. I've always liked his confidence, his ability to become the part.

I insist on traveling by Peace Motors. The other two opt for RTC because their buses get filled up faster. Outvoted, I succumb. Any other time I would have stood my ground and refused to go with them, but with my last days in the country whirling close to the drain, choices seem predestined, and my future, set in stone.

The journey lasts an hour. We alight at a bus park in Owerri and take another bus to Fire Service. Ezeugo reminds us of the wine, so we leave the other commuters waiting for fares along Mbaise Road, and join a rickshaw going to Wutheral, the commercial hub of the city.

After we buy the wine, Ezeugo suggests we go to a tavern for a few drinks, to help us unwind a little, he says. To my dismay, 'Father Nyekachi' is disposed to the idea.

"Think of us as Olympic torchbearers," he says to me. "We are here to brighten another person's home with the warmth that runs in ours. That's how to make a good impression. But right now, I'm not feeling very ... lively. So why not?"

Ezeugo lauds him with a loud chant: Gwam.

"Oh. So the warmth that runs in our home comes from a beer bottle?" I ask, trying to sound indifferent.

"Beer loosens you up," Nyekachi manages to say over Ezeugo's hilarity at my question. "It brings out your fun side. These days when I talk, I preach. I speak in sermons. I didn't use to be so..."

"Dry," Ezeugo finishes.

"I need you responsible," I say.

"If you mean sober, you can relax. I'm not getting drunk," Nyekachi says.

Ezeugo's smirk remains, even after he gulps down his amusement.

"See him," he says to me. "Are you now holier than Father? Or are you now older than the first-born of your father?"

For the second time in a space of hours, I concede. We go to one of those taverns where locals come to watch EPL football matches and pick a table far from the large flat-screen.

Except for the waiter, the place is empty: the live games usually start much later in the day. I would not be caught dead in such a place, but I'm more willing to try new things now, especially as I'm certain a repeat is unlikely.

I like to think of myself as proactive. God speaks to all of us through signs (not outright miracles). And He's gracious enough to give them to me in ample time. If three men go to a bar, common sense should tell one of them to stay sober and watch over the other two. Because, if they all got 'high' at the same time, they could have their pockets picked. The night my roommate returned from a beer parlor and narrated how this had happened to him and his friends, I took it as a sign.

Ezeugo makes a toast. He and Nyekachi raise their mugs to salute me. I return their gesture with my can of Heineken, which I have no plans of finishing and they show their approval with salvos that draw attention to us. They're embarrassing themselves. After the toast, I resume my chat with Ijeoma on WhatsApp.

I type, We are in Owerri.

She types, Where exactly in Owerri are you? I type, In a local bar, drinking to unwind.

She types, What?

I type, Ezeugo's idea. He's treating this marriage introduction like he treats all his job interviews: reduce the pressure of expectation with inebriation.

She types, Okay. But don't stay too long. My folks are waiting. I type, Don't worry. I just worry about our breaths.

She types, LOL. Use lots of breath mint then.

Ezeugo talks about his challenges at work, all the crap he has to take, and how the business of selling clean water, which the government fails to provide, is big business today.

"I was in the bank the other day when this guy came up to me," Ezeugo says, "and asked me if I could help him write in words one million, five hundred and thirty-two thousand naira. He had the figures scribbled on his cheque. I did him the favour and he thanked me. I asked him what kind of business he did and he said he sold packaged water. Imagine that? I've been feeling so sorry for myself ever since. I guess the whole reason my parents sent me to school was to spell six-digit figures for illiterates who cash big cheques."

Nyekachi cackles. I smile.

Ijeoma types, I told you my brother was going to skype your visit so I can be part of it, didn't I?

I type, You did.

Ijeoma types, Well, I'm having a small party here. My friends are with me. And they brought a bottle of champagne with them. Hope you're wearing a bowler hat with your native attire, like a true Ikwerre man.

I type, I'm wearing a three-piece suit, no bowler hat. Ijeoma types, Aw, Chizoba, and adds a sad emoticon.

I type, Kidding, and insert a grinning emoticon. I'll put on my bowler hat when I get there.

Ezeugo says he plans to go into sachet water production. "You won't believe how much profit they make," he says.

I think Ezeugo's business idea is pedestrian. More sachet water means more litter on our streets, and with the government's disposition towards waste management, that's not good. I type 'brb' and slip my phone into my pocket.

"I think it's a shame," I say, "that we're living in a time where most products come in disposables yet the government isn't taking waste management seriously." I rattle off a list of things that come in disposables: sachet water, bottled water, water containers for water dispensers, pepper-sprays, plastic plates, plastic cups...

"Wives," Ezeugo chips in and snickers.

Bereft of words, I stare at him. When I finally come round, I remind him that it was I who, back in senior secondary, refused to vitiate young girls because I knew what I felt for them wasn't deep enough, unlike some persons I know.

"So you had a small prick," Ezeugo says with a smirk. "It's not your fault?"

It's a joke, I know, but I don't find it funny. I have always had a conscience in dealing with people. I'm not some advantage-taker. He knows that. That's my whole point.

I try to stay calm, but it doesn't help that Nyekachi laughed at Ezeugo's quip, so I state the facts—clearly. I remind Ezeugo of his philandering past and how he, and not me, would be in the best position to know all about disposable wives. My tone isn't cheerful, the way his was, but I don't care.

"Stop it," Nyekachi says to me.

I tell him I'm not the one who started it.

"Ezeugo was only teasing," Nyekachi says. "You should try to embrace the funny side of life, sometimes."

"Oh? So saying I use and discard wives is funny to you, correct?" I'm beginning to sound like Ezeugo now.

Ezeugo is giving me a studious gaze, it's his aristocratic squint. He shakes his head as if he is feeling sorry for me before he asks me, "Do you know why you are so intelligent yet you are wasting here?"

The concern in his voice almost makes me answer, but I know he really wants to educate me, not hear my opinion. He allows moments to pass before he says, "Because you are caged in the mind. You don't let yourself go. You have to read meaning into everything, have to see something in nothing, have to always find this in that, always look out for that in this. And if it is there or not there, it says something to you."

He speaks with hand gestures, the upper-class way of saying what I'm trying to express is too deep for words alone.

"But I understood you loud and clear," I say. "You implied that I'm marrying Ijeoma for an Australian visa. What you don't know is, she and I have things in common. For example, we don't believe in accidents. What most people consider accidents we see as signs, and that didn't happen by accident."

"I didn't imply such a thing."

"Liar. Swear on your life."

"I'm sorry you saw something deeper in what I said."

"What did you mean by disposable wives then?"

"Aren't some marriages arranged for the sole purpose of obtaining green cards. Who says I was talking about you?"

Liar. I hate liars. "You think you're smart. You think you can get out of this one. If that's true, then why did you say wives? You could have said disposable husbands."

"Disposable husbands. Happy now?"

I let him know he's full of shit. I let him know his take on me is like analyzing wisdom from the point of foolishness. When I know what I know, how can I go back to ignorance? How can decoding divine messages be a limitation? How did he think prayers were answered?

"I just think you should stop looking for meaning in everything," he says. "Your philosophies have given you pathological aversions to many things."

I laugh at him. He continues to speak, but I'm laughing so hard I can't hear him anymore. I force out tears from my eyes. He's outdone himself this time with his simpleton's simplification of me.

Between gasps and Nyekachi trying to calm the situation, I manage to say, "When you suggested we drink beer before going to see Ijeoma's people, I knew it was a bad idea. And see! I was right."

"But nobody got drunk like you feared," Nyekachi says. "Nobody here lacks a clear head except you."

I call him names. He calls me names too. We raise our voices at each other. I tell him he's always in denial about something and never tired of living a lie. He ought to fill out a U.M.E. form and apply to study law at some university instead of going around saying he's a lawyer, better for him to do something about his situation than pretend he's something he's not. He says I had lived under my parent's roof for too long and here I was, thirty-five and still learning to walk.

"Stop it both of you," Nyekachi barks.

Nyekachi gives us a speech about being family, about building each other and not pulling each other down:

"The general opinion is not necessarily true because the general opinion sees us from the distance of the general public, and always compares us to stereotypes, and judges us by its prejudices. Our relationships make us who we are. The stronger these are, the truer our identity. So let's not tear each other down."

Ezeugo is the one trying to forget who he is, not me. Still, I nod to every word Nyekachi says.

We shake hands, Ezeugo and I. Nyekachi pays the waitress and we leave. I guess we're all delusional in some ways. Life is hard and we're just people trying to cope. Our common struggles unite us. And through these, we build relationships. It will all pass, the resentment Ezeugo and I feel towards each other. When we get to Ijeoma's parents' house, I'll go back to being an engineer. Him, a paralegal. Nyekachi, a reverend father. Maybe, just maybe, the next time we hear a siren, it will tell us something.

STANLEY

He changed his mind about killing himself after his landlord told him to drop dead. He regrets this decision now, standing before a judge who recognizes him, an alumna of his secondary school, likely, since she called him Last Man Stanley, his nickname in those days. She confirms this but tells him not to bother: he won't remember her, she was a shy little student back then while he was a ladies' heartthrob and the life of every school party. She didn't say he was a heartthrob or any of the last part, but he believes it was implied, as only a student of Hussey College Warri in the late seventies would know. He states his name for the court: Stanley Obiki. He's sixty-two, retired, lives in Benin City, worked as a masseur nearly all his life, has never been married, has no child, no close relative, no money, no savings, no pension, which is why he's always late with his rent, and why his landlord is trying to evict him, and why he's suing for harassment.

The defense lawyer asks him why the phone numbers of his work references are either not listed or listed against someone else's name. Like Steven Nelson. And when he says he doesn't know—they might have changed their numbers—the lawyer accuses him of lying in his tenant application. Well. He can accuse him all he likes, but no matter how hard he presses, he'll never admit to being unemployed at the time he filled 'marketing consultant' in the field for occupation, or that he hasn't worked in the last fifteen years, or that for six of those, he had depended partly on handouts from his former co-workers. Steven Nelson is one of the group administrators in his online writing workshop and, in all honesty, he had given Steven's real number, he had just left out the country code for Jamaica.

Apart from sustaining an objection, the woman from his past sits silently through his examination. Her expressions reveal nothing. Stanley finds this a little depressing—he would have been happier if he caught her trying to smother a scoff—because if he's asked to choose between being laughed at by his one-time admirers and being pitied by those who truly care, he'll choose the former: the first scenario motivates; the second, demoralizes. She doesn't seek clarification on his dossier, doesn't want to know the whys or the hows. It's respectful of her. Yes, it is: respectful. But in a demoralizing way.

His day in court ends in a loss and a victory. He's denied the hundred thousand naira he's seeking in damages—for the purported medicines he's had to buy to treat his purportedly elevated b.p., which he alleges was caused by the psychological and emotional stress he suffered on account of his landlord's constant haranguing. His landlord is ordered to desist from any form of verbal or physical attack for the six months he has to evacuate the single-room hovel he rents. He returns to this disputed property in Siluko, a slum in the outskirts of Benin City, where the rain turns the under-repairs road network into a mud slalom, and collapses in his PC chair, the closest chair to the front door. His PC is still on.

It can only mean there's been no blackout since he left in the morning. He finds this worth noting. He has new Facebook messages. Nothing important, just the regular notifications and a few friend requests from people he doesn't know or doesn't want to friend.

He goes through his picture uploads. He looks different in the photos he took less than ten years ago. No wonder women have stopped making passes at him, or giving him glances he couldn't quite call passes because they were done on the sly; they were more like urges to check him out that they were coy about. His job as a masseur at Lagoon Spa had given him access to wealthy, idle women whom he gave massages and sometimes accompanied to exotic getaways, where he experienced the lavish, luxurious lifestyles of the rich (like the night he spent at that yacht beach in Monaco). That life is over now. And all he has to show for it are his photographs and his manuscript, the memoir he plans to publish, the one he posts weekly to his online writing group.

Stanley Obiki won't describe himself as old, just older. He's thinner, skinnier, with baggy eyelids that give him a tired look, true, but his hands are still firm; his facial features, still rugged, although they're beginning to sag a little. He doesn't take selfies like he used to. And even if he did, he wouldn't want to post them on social media. But that's okay since he'll be the only one who still does that; at sixty, his friends are now posting pictures of themselves and their children's families.

He has a new chat on Facebook Messenger. It's Enebeli Gleason-Uduma, the woman he once knew as Summer Rose. She wants him to get on Skype so she can place a video call to him. But he can't make video calls on his PC because his PC doesn't have a webcam.

He types, My... PC... doesn't... have... a... webcam.

What about your phone? Enebeli responds. Do you have a new one, a 4G?

Nah, Stanley types. Still the old one.

Enebeli has been asking him to get a laptop so they can make video calls. He's grateful for his PC and his phone being what they are because he can't let her see him like this. Enebeli was one of his many lovers; she was the one that got away, the one he never quite got over, and it's largely kudos to her that they've maintained their friendship—she makes it a habit to keep him informed on the important happenings in her life: like the birth of Stacy; her marriage to Rick Gleason; the birth of Cassandra and Merlin; the death of her mother; getting her diploma, getting pulled over by the cops, things like that.

Go on, I'm all fingers, he types. Stacy wants to visit Nigeria.

Great. Nice of her to want to know her mother's roots.

Enebeli chose to part ways with him to live in America, more than two decades ago. She lives in New Jersey now, with a husband and three kids.

She wants to meet you, Enebeli types.

Me? Stanley wonders in print. Why me? I'm just curious, that's all. I don't think we've chatted.

It means a lot to her. She's postponed her wedding over it. I'm still confused, Stanley types. She hardly knows me.

Stacy is yours, Enebeli replies with three exclamation marks.

???

She's your daughter. I didn't tell you I was pregnant when I left because I wanted so badly to leave, and I knew it would only give you a stronger argument to convince me to stay. But I couldn't and you know why.

I have lived with this guilt for twenty-five years, Enebeli continues to type. Can you find it in your heart to forgive me? One thing I'm happy about is, I kept our daughter. I kept her even when I knew it would make my immigrant life harder. Believe it or not, it was because I loved you.

Stanley? Enebeli types and his name appears on the screen like a shout. You're taking too long. Say something, she adds.

You loved me? he types.

Yes. I wanted a future with you. The plan was for you to join me. Or have you forgotten?

He remembers. She had sent him money to travel for his visa interviews in Lagos and had kept urging him not to give up on the U.S. visa lottery. But that was until she met Rick Gleason.

I was going to kill myself today, he starts to type, changes his mind, and deletes.

I hate the downslide, he types.

What downslide?

I hate that the best things about my life are in the past.

If you tried to get some rest, you'd disagree.

I was young and vibrant, once.

And narcissistic, and self-centered, and hedonistic. And so many other things.

How does Rick feel about what you're doing? Stanley types.

It was his idea.

Really? He asked you to tell me about Stacy?

Why does that surprise you? But no. He asked me to tell Stacy about you. He's convinced it's the right thing to do. Stacy's getting married soon and as much as he'd like to give her away, he'd feel a lot better if she knew.

He's a good man.

He is.

Were you ever going to tell me? Ever?

If you'd gotten a proper phone, who knows?

Great. Blame it on my phone.

Oh Stanley, please don't make this any harder on me than it already is. Stacy hasn't spoken to me ever since I broke it to her. And unless she needs something from me, like your number or your address, she doesn't call or answer my calls. I told her I don't know your address. I just know you now live in Benin City. She wants to know if it's okay for her to call you. Your daughter wants a relationship with you, Stanley.

I'm a mess right now, a pathetic mess.

I could send you money if you like. Something to help you get ready. How does two thousand dollars sound?

Great. He types 'thank you', but decides it sounds too beggarly, and deletes. I owe you big-time, he types. So when's she coming?

That's up to the two of you. I'll have her call you. That's if she can call you.

Sure she can.

They type their goodbyes and Stanley goes back to Facebooking. Enebeli's chat had interrupted the final perusal he was giving his account before he closed it. He checks his list of friend requests and finds Stacy Gleason. He friends her. Stacy looks a lot like her mother, she's not as fair as her younger sister who is clearly mixed race. She has her mother's laugh, her nose, and her lips. But then... She has lobeless, rather pointy ears. He'll have to give Rick's features another look to decide if they're his. In one picture where Stacy is pouting for the camera, he thinks she has his frown, his facial configuration when he screws up his face. He ponders over all this. She must be his, he thinks.

If there's one thing he doesn't doubt, it's Enebeli needing nothing from him. So why would she lie?

Stanley and Enebeli met in 1982 at Palace Hotel. Or was it Royal Hotel or Hotel Royale? One of those three. Stanley had gone to the reception to ask for his things after he discovered his doorlock had been changed, and Enebeli had come down to inquire about a man she had checked-in with, a man she had rendezvoused and been robbed by while she was asleep. "My jewellery, my phones, my shoes," she said when the manager asked her what items were missing. Stanley remembers that day well. He was supposed to have checked out of his room, but as he hadn't, his paramour, who left days earlier but was still being billed for the room, asked for him to be removed. But for three days he had avoided the hotel staff, sneaking in and sneaking out when the coast was clear. On that fateful day, he had tried his door and found he couldn't unlock it. "Consider yourself lucky your sugar mummy doesn't want to press charges," the manager said to him as he handed him his things. A row ensued between them when Stanley went through his things and shouted, "My Rolex. Where's my Rolex?" The manager called him a liar; there was no missing Rolex because he did not own a Rolex, could not afford a Rolex. They were still wrangling when a frantic Enebeli arrived at the desk.

Stanley returns from his reverie. His screensaver of Nikki Beach, Monte Carlo, at sunset stares at him. He clicks on a file he named 'Living The Life', his autobiography, and scrolls to the last chapter, excited over the new twist in his life and eager to get typing. The new thread in the Enebeli plot promises more intrigue. But then, he could choose to close with Enebeli's phone call (Gloria he calls her in his book) and leave readers guessing how things pan out. One thing he'll want them to feel, is his new disposition, his desire to live, his going from having no reason to wake up in the morning to having something to look forward to: two thousand dollars. And Stacy's visit, of course. Maybe he should just let this story unfold and then decide what to do. It would be a shame to waste a storyline like this. He decides to wait. For now, he'll give his manuscript another revision to put him in the writing mode:

HERE I WAS, OUT IN THE COLD, at the end of my run, and this opportunity was presenting itself. I had just lost my room and she had just lost all her money. We were two lobsters in a cooking pot. The hotel manager asked her if she wanted him to call the police and she said no. I could tell her legs were barely supporting her so I suggested we go sit in the lobby. I let her use my phone. I offered her the little money I had. She said her name was Summer Rose. She was a businesswoman who owned a clothing and interior decorating franchise called Nigerian Versacean. I told her I was a spa manager, I managed Lagoon Spa in the Lekki area for my uncle. We talked for almost two hours before she said good night and retired to her room while I stretched out on the sofa.

STANLEY REMEMBERS SOMETHING he left out about that night: the manager had tried to separate them out of concern for Enebeli's safety. Yes. He had interrupted them with questions a few times too many.

He types, The… manager… came… up… to… us… to ask if she knew me from somewhere, and when she said no, he said, "Madam, you really shouldn't trust strangers so much." He kept coming back to ask if everything was alright. I know he wanted to speak with her in private so he could warn her about me, but the idiot saw the smirks on our faces—I was goofing off and making her smile despite her troubles—and didn't know what to do.

Stanley hears a knock on his door and anguishes 'not now'. He's forced to rise and get the door when the knocks get too loud. Who the fuck...? It's a neighbor, the one who owns the only car in the yard that doesn't need bodywork, a Toyota Camry.

"Oga-sir, is this ya own?" the man asks, holding up a cable, the same cable Stanley had used in shunting electricity from one of the meters.

"No," Stanley says.

"You lie. My son see you the time when you put am. Mister-man, go and pay your bill. Stop parasiting."

Stanley has never heard the word 'parasite' used like that. He imagines his head on the body of a tick perched on top of an electric meter, and marvels at how strong the imagery can be when nouns are verbified. "Are you done?" he asks politely.

"Useless man. You no get shame. Make you run up my meter again, see wetin I go do you."

Stanley closes the door gently on the man's face. He ignores his shouts and returns to his manuscript:

WHENEVER SUMMER CAME TO SEE ME at the spa, the other masseurs pretended I was their boss (and we had laughs). Each time she came, it was hard getting her to go home; she wanted to spend the night. But I kept telling her I had family over, and they would leave soon, but at the moment, I was sharing a bed with a brother.

"My name isn't Summer Rose," Summer said one evening as she prepared to leave. "It's Gloria. Gloria Kadiri."

"Okay," I said. I sort of figured that one out. Nigerians don't give their children names like 'Summer' because we only have two seasons: wet and dry.

"We've been together for three weeks now," she said, "I think it's time we put a stop to the secrets, don't you?"

I agreed. She asked me if there was anything I wanted to tell her, and when I said no, she said, "I know you're not the manager; I've met him."

She said she didn't care if I was a masseur because she really liked me, she liked me and my self-deprecating humor. She said we came from similar backgrounds and my down-to-earthiness was refreshing for her. It reminded her of a time in her life when people were real and you felt like you knew them once you'd met them. It was then I opened up about my past. My parents were so poor that as a child I used to beg to sit on the laps of bus commuters just to get free rides to school, and before I knew it, I had learned how to pick their pockets. I hated being poor. Hated being a nobody. Hated being powerless. And that's what having no money did to you: made you a powerless nobody. I told her I lived for the good days, and by that, I meant days when I could have some of the nice things I want."

She hugged me after hearing this. She held me close. Can't remember when exactly, but it was probably that night that she moved into my small cubicle. And we took our sex life to a new level. She was the best lover I've had, not like the unshapely middle-aged women I'm used to fucking. She was twenty-five, the cover-girl type, great teeth and all, the kind of woman I would be attracted to, not for her money, but because she was very fuckable in every sense of the word.

She stuck with me when things were rough, stuck with me even when she knew I was being a sex valet to some of the guests (she only asked that I use a condom). And when I asked if she was working from home, if she had any money—could she help out with the bills? —she replied, "I'm sorry. There's something else I haven't told you. There are people looking for me," she said. "I'm hiding out here, more or less."

She explained that in her line of work, appearances were everything. The jewellery she lost the night we met was borrowed; they had belonged to her madam and were worth over 2.5 million naira. She was supposed to have handed them over to the driver before she rendezvoused the client, but, tipsy, she hadn't. She said she told me she owned Nigerian Versacean because it was what she was required to say (because then, her lovers would invest in her madam's business instead of trying to lure her into theirs). She had a madam. She was a marketer cum call girl for her madam's franchise. You could say she was a modern-day courtesan specially trained to get at rich, powerful men with weak spots for beautiful women.

"I just need to lie low for a few weeks," she said," until the Agriculture Minister leaves for Texas."

I gave her a curious look and she added, "He promised to include me in his retinue."

His UPS starts to beep and before he can save and shut down, his PC crashes.

"Fuck." He hisses.

From this point on, everything Stanley remembers is patchy. He doesn't remember looking out his window and seeing the outdoor lights of his block of flats crackling with locusts and how that reminded him that that neighbor of his had removed his shunt, and how that now meant everyone had electricity but him, and it would be the same tomorrow and the day after. He doesn't remember stepping out of his door and accidentally kicking the shunt, which his neighbour left on his doormat like an accusing finger. He doesn't remember picking it up and going back inside. Doesn't remember planning to wait till everyone was asleep to replace his shunt, or deciding to do this every night, and each morning, wake up early to remove it before anyone notices. Doesn't remember thinking an opportunity had presented itself when a blackout struck at about 11 pm. He doesn't remember all these because a power surge gave him quite a jolt, erasing his most recent memories. Power was restored and he was electrocuted between the steel burglary protection around the meters that supply his block, which he chose not to unpadlock in his hurry.

HE REMEMBERS HOW BENEDICT HAD EMBARRASSED HIM about not using deodorant and then tried to embarrass him about not wearing underwear (and Benedict knew this because his dick was never packed properly). He was a rustic teenager back then. He had just moved to Lagos to live with Aunt Mabel and since public schools had been his life, he had been blindsided by the cruelty of the private-school kids he met at Stellar Grades Academy, Ikorodu.

"In my family, we don't wear underwear," he bantered. "We've come a long way from loincloths. What will they make us wear next? Rubber?"

"If you like, joke about it," Benedict said. "I'm not saying it to embarrass you. I'm just saying the whole class is tired of seeing your snake sliding around in your trousers. So do something about it."

"Are you sure about that? That's not what Tola told me. If you like I can show you her note."

Benedict studied Stanley's expression. "What note?"

"She passed me a love letter in class and asked that we hook up in the girls' toilet. And we did."

"You're lying."

Stanley showed Benedict, Jelili, and Godwin Tola's love letter, written in her calligraphy, and watched with fascination how they went from his tormentors to his adorers after learning he was banging the daughter of the richest parent in the school, a church minister.

He remembers marvelling at himself that day, but does not remember the big lesson he learned from that incident: how easily he could swing any situation in his favour by saying something that would earn him admiration.

"Cheer up," Stanley says to Enebeli. "True, the things you lost cost quite a lot, but I'm sure I can loan you the money and you can pay me back later."

"You'd loan me that kind of money?" Enebeli asks. "But you hardly know me."

"I pride myself as an excellent judge of character. Let me show you something." He dips his hand into his pocket, pulls out his wallet and from it, takes out a photo he and shows it to her.

"You know who this is?" he asks, pointing at the woman he's embracing in the picture.

"Of course. Everyone knows who that is. It's Chioma Aniweke. The veteran actress."

"We met while vacationing in the south of France. She was going through a difficult period in her life. A divorce. No film roles. I'm responsible for reviving her career."

"How?"

"I talked to a few friends. I barely knew her when I offered to help."

"Wow."

"I think people put too much value on material things. Make a few well-connected friends and your problems are solved. So no more tears, my dear. Now. Let me see that smile."

Enebeli smiled for him.

His teeth chatter and his eyes close. And as he transitions from a multicellular organism to a lifeless conductor, his entire life unravels before him. Most blissful are his memories of his last days with Enebeli, in a suite paid for by the minister so Enebeli could get some rest before her 1 am flight out of the country. The hours had wound down to minutes, the minutes to seconds, and when his run finally ended and he had to say goodbye to the room service, to the pool parties, the elegant people, the breakfast buffets, the lobsters and the seafood menu, the expensive cocktails and the barbecues, the nighttime beach sex and the girlfriend experience, his tears had come like knife stabs and he had wept. He had found it strange and most unlike him. He concluded there had to be a woman for every kind of man and Enebeli was his. With her, it had been the first time he'd felt *electric sparks* and the first time he'd become attached to anyone.

Part One: The Propagandist

His voice is clownishly light for a heavy-boned, strong-jawed man. He drawls through hard-to-pronounce Arabic names and twangs after each maneuver, shifting the way the pitch of a violin changes with less pressure on the fingerboard. I've never given much thought to the features of the American speech pattern until I came to Syria and observed how some locals tried to imitate the way I form words. They weren't trying to be rude, or anything like that. No. Not at all. Just trying to be understood. But none of them was as fluent or as cadenced as this man. I blank out the other sounds in the room—the low roar of conversations, the brief titters of some of the guests, and the banjo playing in the background—and listen to the clinks of crockery, it's a symphony with long spells of surprisingly uniform metre. Returning to my date, who has just shown me his badge, I'm in time to hear him say I will be in direct conflict with my country if I persist with my activities.

A waiter relieves his tray on our table with two whumps: a mug of goat milk for my date and a glass of punch for me. I wait for him to leave before I ask, "How will I be in 'direct conflict' with the United States?"

Jamal (if that's even his real name) tells me Zee-zee, the man I'm after is CIA too. It takes me a while to absorb this, and when my sense of time and place returns, I realize my mouth is open.

"That man ordered my father's... Wait. Are you saying...?"

Jamal shakes his head. He says Zee-zee had no hand in it. There are factions in the Group, cabals. He believes my Iranian 'boyfriend' heads one of such.

I down my drink and flick my tongue like a snake. I asked for punch, so what is this? If they won't put alcohol in punch, why call it 'punch'? It's not really the drink that nettles me, but the way it feels like a second sucker punch. I came here to meet with an insider who promised to give me Zee-zee's whereabouts for a price, and what do I get? An Arab-American spy looking for Taffy.

The year is 2015, eleven months since US-led airstrikes began a cycle of reprisals that have so far resulted in three dead Americans and two British, all of whom were abducted in this country.

Jamal is caramel-complexioned. He has thick-woolly hair bearding his face. His eyebrows look like something a sandstorm disheveled above his eyes, one permanently higher than the other. He says Zalawi is what they call a propagandist, an Islamic religious leader promoting an American agenda in the Middle East. He says the U.S. is in a propaganda war with terrorists, and with Zalawi now at the helm of the Group, they can crush anti-western propaganda and promote their own. The long story short, they dictate the music. He leans back in his chair and lets me mull over his words. He probably thinks I'm thinking what geniuses they are, but I'm actually picturing the look on Taffy's face when I tell him that he once took instructions from America.

He asks me what's funny.

"America running terrorist groups."

He says they're not—running them. They're guiding them. More importantly, they're keeping tabs on them, from the inside.

"Why did Zee-zee invite Lester to interview him?"

He says it wasn't 'Zubi Zalawi' who reached out to my father. Probably one of his aides pretending it was at his behest. He says that they hadn't known my famous father was in Syria until he was abducted. From what he tells me, Zalawi did everything he could to get my father released. "Okay. So maybe it wasn't Zee-zee who lured Lester to Syria with a promise of a rare interview. But even if it wasn't, that doesn't mean he hadn't ordered his execution after he was caught. He could have done it to prove he was no sellout."

Jamal brings his head forward and his voice down. He says some members of the Group weren't happy with the way Zalawi ran things; they were the ones who made an example of Lester to gain the respect of the terrorist community and put their names in the Jihadist Yellow Pages. He says Zalawi forbade Lester's murder, but the faction didn't listen, and that was the deed that splintered the Group.

"So who killed Lester?"

He says he doesn't know, but he won't put it past my Iranian boy-friend, who used to be one of Zalawi's close aides.

I study his beard, taking in their combed lengths, the straightened fluffs of feathery hair hanging at the ends.

He makes me an offer: If I help them, they will help me find Lester's killers.

"Help you do what?"

He gives a long answer to a simple question. From what I can decode, he wants me to report to him, wants me to be his mole.

He asks if I know what 'Tafida Mo'ammar Abbas' is planning next and I'm tempted to interject that Taffy's middle name isn't 'more hammer'; it's 'moo armour'. I don't know what Taffy's planning, and even if I did, I wouldn't tell him. I explain that Taffy is a mere spear-carrier, that I'm the real threat, the Group's mastermind and sponsor, and if I tell him to stop, he will.

He laughs. He apologizes for putting me in a difficult situation and says he is touched by my readiness to take the fall for Taffy. His speech is either conciliatory or condescending, depending on how we'll leave things: if we shake on it, he lets me get up and leave, it's conciliatory. He insinuates that Taffy is using me.

I wrinkle my forehead. "Using me how?"

He says that aside from parading me as a convert who has woken up to the 'evils' of her country, he is mooching off me.

"Are you done yet?"

He isn't (I knew that). He goes on to give me my bio: I'm from Wisconsin. I majored in music and dance in Florida, at the School of Theatre Arts and Dance, and currently teach music and ballet at a middle school in Madison, he forgets the name. I exercise regularly. I love photography. And I'm an amateur film-maker. He says I came to Syria to shoot a documentary to mark one year since my father's execution. I was also looking for a change of environment after breaking up with my cheating boyfriend, my one-time gym instructor. I'm a little surprised by the last part because he couldn't have gotten it from the internet. Why, I haven't even admitted it to myself.

"I'm sorry. Where is all this leading?"

He ignores my question. (Apparently, he's not done with my love life.) He says while shooting my documentary in Dummar, I met and fell for an Iranian chemist trained in Turkey, Mr. Abbas. Even though his tone is friendly it feels like the verbal equivalent of showing me a holstered gun: we know all about you, and yes, know how to hurt you. He tries to get cosy with me by saying he is part-Lebanese, part-Delawarean, but I don't give a rat's ass if he's a Hollywood actor preparing for a movie role as a Taliban cleric, or a redneck with an unusual suntan.

He reaches into his thobe, pulls out a brown envelope, and slides it across the table.

"What's this?"

He wants me to look inside. I pick it up and pull out three photographs. Taffy is in each one. He has his arm around an Arab woman in the first; is laughingly throwing a child up in the air in the second; and is at the wheel of an old model Mercedes-Benz in the third, a covered woman by his side and two youngsters in the back.

Taffy has two wives and five children in Tehran, he tells me.

I flip through the pictures, going back and forth, growing more aware of his eyes. Satisfied, I put them back in the envelope and slide them across. I try to keep a straight face, more embarrassed than shocked—Taffy said his wife died in an Israeli shelling at West Bank.)

"I know about his wives. He told me."

He smirks as if I've just made a joke. Then he banters something about me thinking Taffy would leave his wives for me.

I lash out. I question his timing: Why surface now? For one whole year, the US government said nothing to me, said nothing to my mother.

They didn't think we deserved to know the truth. He tells me to keep my voice down.

"Is it because I'm getting closer to the truth that you now deem it necessary to let me know my father was collateral damage in your fight against terror?"

I say so many things I can't remember what. I bury my face in my hands and sob. I feel hollow, hollow like a percussion instrument. I can hear my heart throbbing in my chest.

He mutters Marion Ursula Ashcroft, and says the U.S. government deeply regrets my loss like it's an official statement. I jerk back my head, indignant, furious. What the fuck? My impassioned speech wasn't a plea for pity. And I'm not looking for his apology either. Right now, if he wants to do something for me, he should just get lost.

"If you don't mind, I'd like to take my leave."

He amuses me with the role he expects me to play. I'm to report anything I learn about Taffy and his splinter group to him. He will find me, he says. Taffy's exact location is not their main concern; they're more interested in his accomplices, his operations, his sponsors, that kind of stuff. Or if he knows anything about the other Americans still being held hostage. He goes over what he expects me to say to Taffy when he asks about our meeting. He warns me not to say I met with an American spy because if I do, Taffy might begin to doubt my loyalty and my life would be in danger. He says it's in my best interest not to appear to have softened on Zalawi. I can always learn the truth about what really happened to my father by snooping around Taffy's video library. Terrorists always keep copies of their executions, all the scalps they've collected.

Fuck him. For people like him, all soldiers from Islamic countries not fighting on America's side are terrorists. Well, Taffy's not a terrorist.

He's a freedom fighter, a mercenary fighting on the side of the oppressed, whether it's against Americans, Israelis, or Turks.

Jamal pulls his chair back and rises, and with a gentle nod, strolls to the exit. I remain in my seat, my lungs returning to their circadian rhythm. I had feared the afternoon would end with him bundling me into a waiting chopper from where I'd be flown to an American military base, where I'll be held until I'm deported.

Does he honestly think I'll switch allegiance just like that? Because I carry an American passport, same as him? Americans. So smug. I'm not surprised, though—that he left me, I mean. I won't exactly say high and dry because I'm the bait now, the worm at the end of his fishhook. What he has accomplished is strapping me to one end, and dipping me in the river. He'll be on alert for any tensions in the line. But how can I betray Taffy? After everything he's done for me? When making my film was proving to be the hardest thing I'd ever tried, along he came and set up interviews for me. And even chauffeured me around. If it wasn't for him, I wouldn't have done those interviews, like the ones I did with the people who last saw Lester before he was abducted, and with those who worked at the local supermarket where he bought groceries. His intervention led to Lester's neighbors, initially unwilling to speak to me, granting me interviews. A sad thing he's married. I had looked forward to breaking the news that I was carrying his child, unsure of how he'd react.

Part Two: The Pantomime

Allah Akhbar!

The pre-dawn call for prayer pierces a twilit Damascus. I stuff my Qatar Airways tickets into my handbag and check the rooms for things

I might be forgetting. Any moment now, I will hear a honk and it will be Ahmed's taxi.

I haven't heard from Taffy since I met with Jamal. I want to stay and finish my film. (Can't keep running every time I get hurt. First Paul, now Taffy.) But I won't. I can't. I have to leave before Taffy tries to reach me. I don't want to be part of a plan to capture him—it's too dangerous. I'm leaving for his sake. And leaving without saying goodbye.

Ahmed arrives at 6:11 am and we set off for the airport. He slips me a black hijab and tells me to wear it. Confused, I obey. He says a Volvo is waiting to take me to 'Mister Abbas' and that when he gives me the signal, I should switch cars as quickly as possible and keep my head down in the other car until the coast is clear.

Ahmed. He's different. He never seemed to me like the type to give anyone instructions. He used to be hesitant, rather diffident; I've never heard him speak so firmly. He was the first real friend I made in Syria. I chose a timorous cab driver, as see-through as spring water, to drive me around the city.

The hood of the taxi rattles like the lid of a steaming kettle as it bumps along the desert road. I wish Ahmed would drive slower, not just for the rattling, but for the dust trail that catches up with us and gasses us each time he takes his foot off the pedal. Heck. My coughing doesn't seem to bother him.

We're in the city's suburbs and the huge rocks on top of the hills look like muffins; they have striations on their sides that remind me of muffins the size of small houses, some sitting dangerously on steep edges. In the backdrop of slate-grey mountains with green 'moulds', a nomad rides on a camel, a young child snuggles against his chest and an almost linear herd of women, children, and sheep trail him on foot.

We go past a few miles of farmland and turn into a gas station. We pull up behind a tan Volvo. A moving truck filling up at the pump across from screens us from the road.

"Now," Ahmed says.

I want to ask, 'What about my stuff in the trunk?', but scramble out of the taxi and quick-walk towards the Volvo and almost collide with an Arab woman moving in the opposite direction. She's wearing the same hijab as me.

I hobble into the Volvo, stretch out in the backseat, and keep my head down. Seconds pass. A minute. The Volvo finally pulls away. It picks up speed and the strong breeze coming through the open windows sweeps up my driver's keffiyeh. My stomach makes stomach noises. Every impulse reaching my brain is telling me to open the door and jump out before it's too late. This could be another kidnap or even worse: I could be heading to my own beheading.

It's a long drive for my anxiety. My driver is silent. There's nothing for me to do but peer out the window and look for foreigners, Americans like me. But all the women I see are wearing burkas, even the little girls. I believe the woman I saw at the gas station had been my decoy. To complete her disguise, she should've worn pants. But she hadn't. It would have been too infidelic of her, too American. Fuck. I'm among strangers. And for all I know, Taffy could be one, too.

The taxi stops at a market, the slaughterhouse district. A cow half-bleats, half-lows in the distance, a grating cry.

Come, the driver gestures.

We weave past beggars who stretch their arms towards us. Some have their fingers missing through amputation. I wonder what happened to them. Were they treated for leprosy? Or is it punishment for stealing? All I know is, I feel sick. The gutters have red in them. Flies perch and pounce around chopping boards, their buzzes getting madder with each meat stall we pass. The air is bad. It teams up with my morning sickness to give me an urge to throw up.

Thwack!

The sound startles me.

Thwack-thwack-thwack.

It's a butcher. He raises his cleaver high up in the air and brings it down on the thin-fleshed bones of a goat littered on his table.

The driver disappears around a corner and I quicken my pace after him. I follow him into a poorly lit bedroom. We move from room to room, rooms that wreak of the cheap camphoric perfume locals like to wear. We pass several doors and enter a windy alley that leads to a court-yard, which I can tell, from the pots stacked on one side and the aroma of atayef, is an open-air kitchen.

Something snags my neck. A washing line. I step back and duck under it. The courtyard looks recently swept: there are fresh broom-marks on the floor and a heap of peanut husks in one corner. A hen clucks to warn me I'm getting too close to her brood. The driver ushers me into yet another room, a parlor. A giant-size cathode-ray TV sits on a low desk, and on top of it is a VCR. A desk drawer juts out just enough to reveal its contents: videotapes. The driver signs 'wait here' and disappears behind a curtained door.

Taffy strolls in minutes later. From the sand on his forehead, where he has a slight prayer bump, I can tell he has just finished saying his Salat al-Fajr. He hugs me and calls me 'Sweet Marion', the pet name he gave me. I hug him back, surprised at my stiffness. I've never been like this when I'm with him. I'm nervous and I fear he can sense it too, so I say, "My luggage. They took my luggage."

He assures me I have nothing to worry about; my things are safe. He asks why I'm leaving so suddenly, and I reply that I've finished my documentary and since I hadn't heard from him, I feared something might have happened.

He asks if I met with the informant.

I swallow before I reply, "I did. But it was one of Zee-zee's men warning you to flee Syria for your own good." What's wrong with me? Those are not my words.

He cusses in Arabic. He pulls me close, kisses me on the forehead, and then lightly on the lips.

He asks if we discussed anything, if he showed me anything. Jamal didn't say how to respond to that.

"Like what?"

He says I should think hard.

"No."

He cradles my face and lets his hands slip to my neck, massaging my throat and communicating glimpses of their strength. He asks me if he showed me anything, anything in a brown envelope.

"You had me followed?"

He slaps me. Grabs me by the hair and flings me onto the couch.

"He showed me pictures," I yell, "pictures of you and your family. You lied to me. I can't believe you lied to me!"

He stops and stares. His eyes glaze over with new awareness. He asks if I'm hungry.

"No thank you."

My left ear sings like a tuning fork. He comes to my side and kneels beside me. He rubs my burning cheek. I push away his hand. He says he's sorry.

"I want to go home. It's not safe for me here, not safe for us. I'm not mad at you anymore. I wish you a happy life."

I don't think he hears me because he starts telling me how much he loves the hazel color of my eyes, and how much he loves being with me. Finally, he talks about his wives.

He married both on the same day. They were gifts from a sheik, his daughters. He had to accept or else it would have been a slight. He doesn't love them, he says, never loved them, will never love them as much as he loves me, he says.

"Why did you lie?"

He says he planned to tell me about them, eventually, but first, he wanted me to fall for him so hard that I'd consider being his third, so I'd consider living the life of the wife of a Mujahedeen.

I shake my head. I hope my gesture says it's so wrong to do that to people.

He says he's ready to leave his wives if that's what I want. He says he loves me. Only me.

"And your kids?"

He says he loves his kids too and smiles at his joke.

His kids are still very young, he says. They need their mothers more at this age.

"I want to help you find Zee-zee, but after that, I'm done." I sound convincing, even to myself.

He asks if I'm still leaving for America.

Really? Is he really asking me this? Look at the time. Has it crossed his mind that I might have missed my flight? "I don't know. "

He says he's sorry in Farsi: Maazerat mikhaam.

He hugs me. It's settled; he thinks we're good. He tells me he has news that will blow my mind. He says it's better if I sit down. I remain standing.

Two days ago, he says, his men captured five American soldiers fighting on Zee-zee's side. Zee-zee is an American spy, he declares.

"You're kidding," I say and cup my mouth to hide my mechanical expression.

He says the worst is still to come: my father had uncovered the truth and my country had taken care of him by handing him over to radicals because they couldn't trust him with such a secret, especially as he was a reporter.

I gape at him. A century passes. I don't need to fake my surprise this time. My next words hang like a wattle on my throat: Are you sure?

He gives me a look that speaks volumes, and I crumble to the couch and bury my face in my hands. I scream. I cry. I spew out my pain until it hollows me. He sits down on my right and traces a finger up my spine. He uncovers my hair and runs his fingers through my thick silky tresses.

I nudge him away. "I'd like to be alone."

He obliges me. His footsteps recede. The curtained door opens and I hear the clinks of cutlery in the next room before it shuts.

I miss home. I miss my mother. I miss the Madison skyline. I miss biking down State Street Saturday mornings. I miss eating Babcock ice cream while I'm biking.

I'm awake but I'm not here. I have blackouts when I'm scared. Something about the way I'm feeling right now reminds me of my first pantomime.

I was four. Nola Rae was performing. She was a giant toy dancing to percussions that dictated her mood. She looked like she was hanging by strings, the way she slumped forward and hooked her arms in the air by the elbows. She stayed in that position, jerking her arms up and down, mimicking a pull from above. At the end of her dance, she wound down like a piece of clockwork and remained motionless until the lights went out.

Her face, even though a clown's, was rather frightening for a four-year-old: a whiteface that brought out the yellow of her teeth and the not-so-white white of her eye; the dark lips that grinned plastically; the punk-rock eye makeup that combined with the whiteface to make her look deathly.

I was standing near the stage with a group of other children roughly my age. I had seen Nola approach and seen the other kids running. And although I wanted to run (and there had been plenty of time to), I couldn't move. I became a petrified volunteer in Nola's next act. I looked on as she covered my nose with a hanky and plucked quarters from my nostrils, after a rude nose fart that had the audience laughing. Nola turned me into a vending machine and took out quarters from different parts of my body and handed them to me, much to my bemusement and the crowd's delight. I had felt used. It's the same feeling all over again. Except, this time, I'm not a vending machine. I'm more like Nola. I'm a giant doll being stringed by two puppeteers: Jamal and Taffy. I'm Marion the Marionette. It's just as well if I were hanging from strings.

The desk drawer catches my eye. The videotapes. I go over to them. Running a finger along the length of a stack, I check the labels. Many of them are in Arabic. A few are in French. Nothing in the first drawer. I open the second. French and English names here: 'Deschamp', 'Smith', 'Carmichael', 'Lisaresseux'.

'Ashcroft'.

The name assaults my nervy composure.

Someone's behind me. I spin around. Taffy. He's watching me quietly. Going by the distance between him and the curtained door, he didn't just walk in.

He asks what I'm doing.

"What's this?" I hold the tape to his face so he can see the label on it. I wave it like a weapon, my arm shaking, my body language saying 'don't come near me'.

He says he made a copy of my film. "Why?"

He says he wanted it as a reminder of the time we fell in love.

The floor is suddenly uneven. My head hurts. I hear pantomime percussions. He's giving me a quizzical look, watching me as if I were unwell. Another jolt rocks me. His image rolls sideways like meat on a skewer.

He asks if I'm okay. I don't respond.

He says if I like, he can show me. He says it in that cool manner I've always found relaxing and reassuring. It was therapeutic then. It's terrifying now.

He takes the tape from me, goes to the VCR, slots it in, and turns on the TV. He has his back to me. It's my chance. I make for the door, dawdling at first before charging and slamming into it. I turn the knob. It won't open. And there's no key in the keyhole. I try the knob again. This time I pull it towards me. And it creaks. And it opens. I don't wait, I rush out. I run past onlookers who just stare at me as I bump past. I run for the life in me (run with the life I'm carrying), run in any direction that first catches my eye, a scream on my lips for anyone who might try to grab me. All I know is, if my legs carry me to safety, it'll be about time.

How Hamisu Survived Bad Kidneys
and a Bad Son-in-Law

There is always a story behind a story. And sometimes, a story behind that too. The goal-driven people that we are, our efforts are often geared towards ensuring our lives go as planned, or that we survive the many plots against us. Whether we are planners who look out for our- selves or plotters who deny others with counter-goals, when you think about it, it is really just a matter of semantics. Life is a vicious contest. Not everyone can win. Especially when winning involves undermining others. (I do not like to use the word 'undermine' because it makes me think of 'underworld'.) The fact is, ultimately, it is Allah Al Fattah who blesses a man's plot, and I speak not only of his farmland.

If this were my story, it would have been about how I took another man's wife. If this were not my story, it would have been about why polio still exists in the world despite concerted global efforts to eradicate it. But since the story behind those two paints a clearer picture, perhaps I should tell that one.

It began on a Saturday, and as it was with most Saturdays, I was at Kawo General Hospital to see my usual points-of-call. First on my list was a man I had visited once before. He was a convict, a man who had been brought in from Narayi Remand Home so he could receive proper medical attention, at an affordable cost, while he underwent weekly haemodialysis at a private clinic that had a dialysis machine, somewhere in Angwar Sarki, I was told. I peered inside his ward and saw he was still asleep and considered leaving, but chose instead to seat myself in the chair beside his bed and study my Qu'ran. It was during my meditation that I noticed his eyelids flutter (they fluttered more than once), and I immediately knew he was awake and refusing to get up or let me know he was awake. I called him by his surname, Hamisu, but he kept still. Almost. The fingers on the hand resting open-palm on the bed twitched a little.

It was a coughing fit that brought him out of his surveillance. Alarmed by the way his head kept lolling forward with each spasm, I grabbed the bottled water on his bedside table and poured him a cup. After several gulps, he laid back down and grated a thank you. He looked at me for a while and then said, "Imam Ibrahim, why do you still visit me? You can see for yourself that I am not about to die—at least not yet. I am sure, if you looked around, you will find others in greater need."

He had just spoken to me as the imam assigned to the hospital, as a cleric whose duty it was to console the bereaved and make sure the dying said the Shahaadah. His words translated, kindly leave me alone, but underneath it all, I heard a different request, a cry for help: Your visits are perfunctory. I need a friend.

I sank back in my chair and said, "Mallam Hamisu, true, you are alive, and true, too, that this is likely to continue, insha Allah. Unfortunately, what I see when I look at you is a different kind of death. This one is not physical in nature. And as your brother, I will not leave until you tell me what is wrong."

A beady teardrop crawled to the cliff of his temple and zipped down to his ear. He tightened his eyelids and wrung out the tears in them.

"Is it Safiya's wedding?" I asked. "She is young, yes, but surely you must derive comfort in knowing that if anything happened to you, Allah forbid, she will be in good hands."

His forehead grew creases when I said this and his right hand clenched.

Mention the name Lawal Hamisu and the locals will tell you about a man whose greed led him to betray his people. Mention the name Imam Jubril in the presence of Lawal Hamisu and you could almost give him a stroke. Suffice it to say, up until then, I could not understand how having Imam Jubril as a son-in-law could elicit such a reaction from a man in Hamisu's social standing. I had always seen Imam Jubril as an honourable man, a man of considerable means. He was a man whom I looked up to as my superior, the chief cleric of Kawo Central Mosque. But I soon learned, with great shock, that Imam Jubril was not all he seemed.

BEFORE 2002, BEFORE THE PROTESTS over the Miss World Pageant that the country was set to host turned violent, Imam Jubril had watched, with indignation, as immigrants bought up land in his home district of Kawo and built edifices. A blasphemous article published in a national daily led to an ugly backlash from angry Miss World protesters. The bloody riots that ensued provided the tinder they needed to force foreign settlers to flee. As a result, rent and the cost of buying a home plummeted and Imam Jubril was able to buy a five-bedroom bungalow at a giveaway. Post-riot, Kawo saw a fall in the price of goods. I remember how I had bought a set of couches for a ridiculous sum from a desperate homeowner trying to cut his losses as he prepared to resettle in the south of the city. At the time, order had been restored and the looting of shops owned by settlers had stopped. It was during this period that Imam Jubril instructed all locals not to buy homes belonging to settlers unless they went for next-to-nothing. So when Lawal Hamisu, a local housing agent, was brought before him, accused of helping a non-local sell his house for a fair price—not just selling it for a fair price, but selling it to a fellow local—everyone wondered what sort of example Imam Jubril would make him.

THE COURTHOUSE WALLS ARE SMUDGED. There are no pictures on them. No portraits of the president and the state governor, as you would expect to find in most government offices. What you see when you look at the walls, besides the smudges, are common house geckos and ant cracks. The room is crammed with people and they have formed a semi-circle around Hamisu. Imam Jubril sits alone at one end of the room, behind a long table. Judging from his freshly carved sideburns, he has just had a trim using a razor-sharp knife and shaving cream. He seems to disapprove of facial hair above his upper lip, yet he does nothing about the tiny strands of hair sticking out of his nose. But of course, Hamisu is too far away to observe this. What he sees are the pitted scars on Imam Jubril's face, a severe case of acne that has left his face rubbery and permanently caked in pockmarks like the court walls' coarse finishing.

"I did not know who owned the house, I swear," Hamisu says. Someone in the courtroom shouts liar and it charges up the crowd.

Imam Jubril appeals for calm and then says to Hamisu, "It does not matter whether you knew who owned it or not. If you had done your homework, you would have known. But you were greedy. The higher the cost of the house, the higher your commission, not so?"

Hamisu shakes his head, more from fear than denial. "So I will punish you," Imam Jubril says firmly.

"Please. My wife is sick and my children are still young."

"You are lucky I believe you acted out of greed, and not the intention to side with an immigrant against your brother, or else I would have had your body buried neck-deep in sand and your head trampled on by horses. You are lucky. I will spare your life."

"Where is your gratitude, traitor?" Imam Mainasara barks at Hamisu, and Hamisu snaps out of his daze and throws himself at Imam Jubril's feet.

"Since you have chosen to abuse the trust laid upon you," Imam Jubril says to Hamisu, "from this day forth, you will cease to work as a housing agent in this community. Any landlord you continue to service will be courting my wrath and the wrath of this community. Find a new line of work or leave Kawo."

For the next three months, Hamisu offloads trucks that bring goods to the market. He becomes a pepper picker so he can have more time with Maimuna, his sick wife, but soon turns to shining shoes when work is hard to find.

ONE AFTERNOON HE RETURNS HOME to find his youngest daughter Nafisah all alone in the house, and when he asks where the rest are, she tells him that Maimuna's condition got so bad that the neighbours rushed her to the general hospital, Safiya and Laraba went with them. Hamisu gathers all the money he has in the world—a hundred and fifty naira—and takes Nafisah and a rickshaw to the hospital. Young Nafisah is silent all through the ride. The situation with her mother has taken a toll on her. Her reticence makes her seem much older than her four years and three months.

Hamisu and Nafisah head straight to the reception when they reach the hospital. There, they are directed to the GOPD, and when they get to the waiting lounge at the GOPD, they find familiar faces from their street. Their neighbours are gathered in a circle around Maimuna, who is stretched out on the floor. Mairo Mai Dawa stands over Maimuna and fans her with her wrapper, putting more vigour into it than she ever did with the piece of cardboard she used in fanning the charcoal fire that she roasted corn over. Hamisu learns from Al-Amin that the attendant behind the counter insisted that they purchase a hospital card, and they have done that. And then he insisted that they pay the emergency charge for Maimuna's treatment, and they have done that. Now he is insisting that they pay for a hospital bed. "Since we got here, it has been get this, get that. Bring money here, give money there. It is just too much. This is not how to handle an emergency, saboda Allah," Al-Amin laments.

Hamisu tries to appeal to one of the nurses, but she is talking at the same time and not listening to him. So he clamps her by the shoulders and steers her into a corner to plead with her. The attendant rushes to the alarmed nurse's aid and shoves Hamisu aside. "Be careful," he warns. Hamisu's neighbours do not like the way the attendant pounced on Hamisu and pushed him away. They do not like his brash and uncompromising attitude. They surround him with questions: Are you mad? Have you lost your mind? Is that how to behave? The attendant crouches low and tries to shield his head from the spindle-like arms that hurl open palms at his face. He does not want to run because that will require turning his back on them, and does not want to fight back because that might worsen the matter, and does not want to apologize, beg, or cry because that will humiliate him and give them satisfaction.

"Stop," Hamisu yells at his supporters. "Leave him alone. How does beating him help Maimuna?" He turns to the nurse he jacked roughly against the wall and says, "I'm sorry. Please help my wife, matron."

"The doctor can't see her like this," the nurse says, "Look at her. She's in a critical state. You need to buy the items that we'll need to manage her condition. You have to buy it. Begging will not solve anything. Killing us won't either."

"Wicked people," Mairo says. "What is the money we paid you for Emergency meant for? You should have told us this before making us pay for all those other things."

"It is for getting a specialist here on time. We have procedures."

"To hell with you and your—"

"Enough," Hamisu yells. "Hajiya Mairo, please stop. This is getting us nowhere."

"Why did you wait so long to bring her here?" another nurse asks rhetorically. "She did not get like this overnight. You people fail to do the right thing at the right time and then you come here acting like it's all our fault."

"Yi hakuri. We are sorry," Hamisu says. "Please help us."

"I do not need your 'sorry'. I am only sorry for her."

A third nurse gives Hamisu a sheet of paper. It is a list of items Maimuna needs urgently. "You can buy them at the pharmacy outside the gate," she says.

Hamisu receives two thousand naira from his neighbours, the

remainder of the money they had raised in his absence, and thanks them with tears in his eyes. "Just hurry," they tell him. "Go."

But Maimuna's breathing is laboured and Hamisu does not like the sound of it. He does not want to leave her side just yet. He considers giving the money to Al-Amin. But will his best friend run like his life depends on it? Reluctant, Hamisu sets off for the pharmacy. When he returns, there are strange faces in the GOPD lounge.

Only the attendant and one of the nurses he met earlier are familiar. "They have moved her to A and E," a nurse tells him before he can ask.

"Where is that, please?"

They point him down a narrow corridor with patients sardined on benches lining opposite walls so they are either sitting side-by-side or facing one another, and tell him to follow it to the end, take a left, and look straight ahead, he cannot miss it.

At most hospitals, bawling children are a constant feature, especially around the injection room. But the wails Hamisu hears reverberating around the corridors as he weaves around corners and pushes past people do not sound like children. Driven by a sudden fear, he rams through the double-swing doors with the sign 'Accidents and Emergencies' and finds himself in a general ward.

His neighbours are crowding around a bed. Mairo sees him and bursts into tears. Laraba runs to him shouting 'Mama is dead, Mama is dead,' as if she expects him to do something about it. Stunned, he drops the bag he is carrying and the I.V. fluid in it rolls onto the floor and spins to a halt. He sees Safiya slumped on the floor, her back to the wall, looking lost as she watches him, tears streaming down her cheeks. His heart beats and misses. And then it pulsates. Embraces come and go. 'Allah has given, Allah has taken'. 'Be strong for your children's sake'— someone whispers in his ear. Bodies ebb back to allow him through, but he does not move. He just stands there staring at the shape on the bed, dreading the reality of what so far seems a bad dream. Nafisah throws herself on the bed and sobs against the shape, her head sideways on its chest, occasionally looking up to see if it wakes. Someone tries to pull her away, but she fights him off. "Kabani, leave me," she pleads. When blood returns to Hamisu's cranial shores, he stomps to Nafisah, pulls her to him and crushes her against his chest, holding her tight until her tear-convulsions become his.

OVER THE NEXT SIX YEARS, Hamisu's daughters go from under-sevens to pre-teens. The eldest, Safiya, is ripening fast like pawpaw perched up a tree, ready to fall when the time is right. She is lanky with small, roundish hips, and is tall for her age, and has skin the colour of the palm of my hand: cocoa butter. Her nose is Fulani-Arab and delicately contoured, lengthy in bone, and pleasantly full-blown on her face of a child. She and her sisters are out hawking groundnuts one morning when Imam Jubril sights them. He stops to stare at Safiya. For a short spell, he forgets where he is: outside the mosque, listening to his pupils recite verses from the Qu'ran. He heaves his bulk off his mat, instructs his pupils to go on without him, and follows the three groundnut sellers to an electronics shop, where they have joined a group of other kids watching a wrestling match showing on a television on display.

"Kai, yarinya," he shouts to the tallest one.

It takes several shouts to get their attention. And when they finally hear him, they race each other to get to him, a game of beat the rest to the buyer. But Imam Jubril does not care about rewarding the winner with a sale. Nor does he care about their groundnuts; he has other interests.

He says to the eldest, going by her height and general appearance, "Come. I like your groundnuts. They look ready. I hope they will be soft and pink on the inside when I crack them open."

Still tittering with her sisters, Safiya nods. She lowers her tray to her nubby chest and the rolled-up piece of cloth on her head (the cushion for the tray) unravels and flops down over one-half of her face. She hides her eyes and holds up the tray for him to see the twenty-naira heaps of ground-nuts collected into old evaporated milk tins with their tops removed.

"What is your name?" Imam Jubril asks her, clutching a fistful of groundnuts.

"Safiya."

"Who is your father?" "Mallam Lawal Hamisu."

Of course, Imam Jubril exclaims in his heart. She is Hamisu's little girl. My, has she grown. What a beautiful creature she is turning out to be. Hamisu would be a fool not to know that she is his ticket out of poverty; she can easily be exchanged for wealthy in-laws.

"How old are you?"

"Twelve. I will be thirteen in a few days."

"Good. You are a big girl." He tastes a few boiled groundnuts and buys two tins.

THE NEXT DAY, Imam Jubril is pacing around the entrance of the mosque, waiting for Hamisu to arrive for his Fajr Prayer. He retreats into the mosque when he gets tired of having to respond to every arriv-er's greeting, some of whom suddenly develop something to discuss. He tells the Al-Majeris who sleep in the mosque to alert him when Hamisu surfaces. Hamisu is hardly ever late, but most times, rather than enter the mosque, he prefers to worship in the open-air prayer ground reserved for latecomers.

Hamisu arrives at fifteen minutes to prayer-time. He goes straight to the tap and crouches in front of it, preparing to perform his Wudu. He has a small swelling on his neck, a goitre, and is so thin that his caftan looks over-sized. He turns on the tap and it makes a gurgling sound before a rude gush.

Imam Jubril picks his moment. He strolls over to Hamisu and they greet in salaam. He tries to make small talk but realizing he is perplexing his listener with his sudden interest in him, says, "Your daughters will be needing husbands soon. I can help you with that."

"Thank you, Imam, but I want them to gain admission into the university, first."

"University? But where will you get the money for that? Can you even put them through secondary school?"

"Allah will provide."

"Allah will provide them with husbands, that is what He will do, and they will take care of their education."

"Husbands will promise and they will fail. You cannot put your faith in men, only in Allah and His mercies."

"Listen to me. I know the right men for your daughters. Trust me, Mallam Hamisu. Those who have put their faith in me can testify that I have never disappointed them."

Hamisu guzzles water from a plastic kettle, holds some in his mouth, and slips in a finger to scrub his teeth. After a few squeaks, he spits out the gargle, relaxes his cheek muscles, and says, "No thank you, Imam."

"But there are many bad elements in our universities, lecturers and students alike. If your daughters are married first, they will know well to steer clear. Or do you want your girls coming home with bastards?"

"I want them to never have to depend on any man."

More worshippers arrive and as the walls grow ears, Imam Jubril decides it is time to leave the matter. 'Qaddara ya riga fata', he declares, and retreats into the mosque, convinced that Hamisu has spoken out of spite. It is common knowledge that you do not send your daughters to school because your investments will only profit another man, another family. It is better to betroth them as soon as they start to menstruate and allow your in-laws to contribute their quota, and if that amounts to taking your daughters into their homes and into their beds, then so be it.

I REMEMBER THE COMMERCIAL Hamisu talked about. It had aired several times on the local station. The girl in it was Safiya, it turned out. I did not know her then; we first met at the hospital. She had looked divine with her lips darkened to match pupils that danced in glistening pools of white as she expressed her satisfaction with staying dry with Always sanitary pad. Hamisu said the commercial had upset Imam Jubril. I tried to imagine why. There had been nothing salacious or offensive about it. Yet, Imam Jubril had called a meeting of the chief imams in Kawo over it.

SAFIYA'S COMMERCIAL DOES NOT SIT WELL with Imam Jubril. He is convinced that Hamisu plans to make a public spectacle of his daughter to attract the wealthiest suitors. He discusses Hamisu's action in permitting Safiya to make an exhibition of herself with a few friends and speaks with so much passion, and at so much length (at too great a length) that his friends begin to wonder what exactly infuriates him.

Imam Jubril summons the chief imams in Kawo to a meeting, and at the meeting, he laments how Hamisu is teaching his daughter to leave her hair uncovered and parade herself in front of cameras like those foreign beauty queens they had driven out of the country. He posits that Hamisu is destroying both her sense of humility and her sense of decency. The more he speaks, the more he is convinced that his real motive is to protect Safiya from her irresponsible father.

The council of chief imams summons Hamisu to its meeting. They accuse him of polluting his daughter's head with western ideologies, of pushing her in a direction alien to good Muslim women. All for money. Hamisu begins by thanking them for their concern and for their good intentions, and for summoning him to a dialogue aimed at a resolution in his daughter's best interest. He then asks them if a woman's sanitary pad was now a 'western ideology'—or is it shooting a commercial?—and they prevaricate to their fears that Safiya might advertise condoms next, and how that could unleash the pigeons of fornication in the locality. They ask him if he will be a proud father if he saw Safiya's face on the packs of condoms, and they mistake his quandary on how to respond—he is wondering how their discussion had segued to this—for a sign that he had seen his guilt. They call him a bad parent, a widower unfit to raise women.

That warning goes unheeded. Safiya appears in yet another commercial. This time it is a short video clip to create awareness for polio. In it, she asks the public to avail themselves for an upcoming immunization exercise. Enraged by Hamisu's defiance—for yet a second time—Imam Jubril comes up with a plan that will settle Hamisu's hash.

IMAM JUBRIL SITS ALONE fingering his prayer beads after Maghrib Prayers. Watching as worshippers troop out of the mosque, he waits for Hamisu to leave too, and when he does, he calls those still around to come together so he can make an announcement.

"It has come to my attention," he says, "that America plans to release a deadly plague on our community under the guise of immunizing our children."

"La illah," Mallam Bature laments, crossing his forearms behind his head.

"They will not succeed," Bala Mai Direba says. "We will not allow it."

"Let's hope so," Imam Jubril says. "Because, as we speak, they have already set their plan in motion."

"How? What plan?" Kaza-Kaza asks.

"We have traitors among us," Imam Jubril says. "Let me allow Mallam Yero to tell you what he has already told me. Yero!"

Yero rises from his mat and describes how he had eavesdropped on a conversation between Lawal Hamisu and three Red Cross officials, white people, at the end of which, Hamisu had received a bribe to carry out infanticide.

"Lawal Hamisu?" Imam Mainasara tightens his jowl. "Lawal Mai Shoe-shiner?"

"Kwarect," Yero confirms.

"Is it not his daughter's picture we see on those polio awareness billboards?"

"It is," Imam Jubril says.

"What a devil." Imam Mainasara palms his fist. "Even after you forgave him, he does this."

"Once a traitor, always a traitor."

"Yes. Once a money-loving ingrate, always a money-loving ingrate." A mob marches to Hamisu's house and wrenches him from his distraught family. Hamisu is jailed. His daughters are put in an aunt's care, Rahila is her name. Men come to Rahila seeking Safiya's hand in marriage. She is the bad one, they tell her, the one who needs the firm hand of a good Muslim husband. Even Rahila's womenfolk think the men are right. Eventually, she succumbs. Safiya is betrothed—to Imam Jubril, whom everyone agrees is the best man for the job.

But Imam Jubril is not celebrating yet. He worries that Hamisu could be released from prison in time to stop his wedding. And as he battles to find a new plan, Fate presents him with one in the shape of a BBC reporter who has been pestering him for an interview. The foreign news correspondent is covering a story on the origins of the rumours that fueled the northern boycott of polio immunizations in the country.

THE INTERVIEW HAD AIRED ON STATE RADIO. I missed it, but my next-door neighbour, Karim, did not. By his own account, the interviewer had tried to distract Imam Jubril from the real issue by floodlighting his personal life, namely, his ongoing plans to marry Safiya.

"I UNDERSTAND THAT YOU RECENTLY PROPOSED MARRIAGE to the girl in the polio ad," the reporter says, "and that the man you accuse of betraying your people so happens to be her father. Am I correct in saying that this man is against your marriage to his daughter?"

"You will have to ask him that. I will not speak for him."

"Did you frame this man so you could marry his daughter? Was that your ulterior motive?"

"How would you have known my motive if it was all interior? I do my things in the open. And I do not have to frame it for all to see. There was nothing interior about my marriage proposal."

"The girl's father is currently in jail. Isn't that what you wanted, sir? For him to be out of your way?"

"Am I the one who exchanged my conscience for the almighty American dollar? You are a foreigner. I do not expect you to understand how a reputation like his can ruin his family, how it can destroy his children's future. But understand this: it is because of me that things can be different for them."

"Can you explain how? Just so there are no assumptions?"

"Becoming her husband makes me her family. And as her family, her problems are my problems. I cannot... er..."

"Shirk your responsibilities."

"No. That is not it. I cannot shy away from my responsibilities no matter the circumstance."

"So, you are saying, in essence, that when you become her husband, you will be willing to help her father regain his freedom?"

"Of course, why not?"

The interview leads to international calls for Hamisu's release. President George W. Bush cites Hamisu's predicament in a speech about ending poverty and low literacy in certain parts of the world to prevent them from becoming fertile grounds for breeding anti-western sentiments.

When the people of Kawo hear this, they say to one another, "Oh, so the US president wants to make us infertile?" and are even more convinced of Hamisu's treachery.

It is exactly the turn of events Imam Jubril had hoped when he granted the interview. Hamisu remains behind bars and Imam Jubril makes Safiya his third wife.

BETWEEN SOBS, Hamisu informed me that Imam Jubril had stopped

Safiya's schooling and that he had made it clear to her that he wanted her to have his children and stay home and look after them.

His tearful effusion worked like a balm on his low spirits. By the time Safiya, Laraba, Nafi, and 'Umi' (Rahila) arrived with his breakfast, he was cheerful and willing to eat.

At a few minutes past one, Safiya looked at her watch and worried that she would get into trouble if she did not leave for home immediately: Imam Jubril forbade her from spending a minute over two hours outside his house.

"Before you leave," Hamisu said to her, "can you go to the pharmacy and get me a new supply of iron tablets, Iro-Plex?"

"But you've not finished the one you have," Safiya replied.

"What if there is a shortage? What will I do then? It is good to stock up, especially in places like this where they only give you Panadol."

"Shikena, I will go."

Hamisu turned to me and said, "Mallam Ibrahim, can you drive her?"

"There's no problem, Baba," Safiya said quickly.,"I can get there on my own."

"It would be my pleasure," I said.

"Go with him," Hamisu said to Safiya. "You will get home faster that way. He can drop you off a short distance from your house so Imam Jubril does not see the two of you together."

I live in Manchester now. When I think back to that day, I realize that Hamisu had sent Safiya and me on our first date. A 'date' is what they call it here. She was fourteen at the time. And although I wanted to, I did not court her. I was more concerned about her welfare, with giving her courage—and contraceptives.

Imam Jubril's BBC interview had backfired in the end. It had given Hamisu the media attention he needed and had led to several donations that took care of his medical expenses and his trip to India for a trans-plant. I got to know him better during those bed-ridden months, and I can tell you with a fair amount of certainty that he hated injustice. He was a man who wanted fairness and equality for everyone regardless of their tribe, gender, creed, or social class. (And it might have been true that he had helped that non-indigene to sell his house for what it was worth. I never asked him about that.)

He donated a sizeable portion of his largesse to the borehole-water project in Kawo and that set many minds thinking: Could this man truly be as rapacious and as treacherous as they say? Yero recanted his testimony about seeing him with Red Cross officials, but he did not implicate Imam Jubril. Imam Jubril decided it was time for them to settle their differences and came to see him in the hospital, one morning. I cannot forget his visit. He came with watermelons but had to flee when Hamisu took them and turned them into cannonballs aimed at his head. I was the one Hamisu sent to him with a request that he allow Safiya to go with Hamisu to India, as she was to be his kidney donor. Imam Jubril had seen this—Hamisu's first recognition of him as Safiya's husband—as a move towards friendship and had said yes. It turned out to be the final piece in an escape plan. Safiya did not return with her father and Imam Jubril learned the hard way that the man he falsely accused of being a traitor was capable of treachery if it was to save his daughter, most fathers are, and that a man like me, regarded as devout by most, could be used to carry out such deceit.

Safiya sought and was granted asylum in the U.K. She had her marriage dissolved. (If you are legally a minor at the time you are wed, you can have your marriage annulled. That is the law here.) After completing her high school education in Glasgow, Safiya went on to study journalism at the University of Manchester, graduating in 2013, the same year we got married, which was also her first time in the country since 2004.

Imam Jubril tried to start another rumour, something about keeping Africa impoverished so that rich nations can seduce our women and spread their foreign seeds. Unfortunately for him, the people of Kawo knew something he didn't, something he would later find out and come to my father's house to heckle him about. Today, the locals still hear him but no one listens. I think he learned how to cope with being considered senile long before he actually became senile.

Presently, Safiya works for Searchlight, a relatively new cable network TV station in Nigeria with global ambitions—she is their UK correspondent and she hosts a show about the plights of economically disadvantaged people, Voice For The Voiceless. Inspired by my late father-in-law (and funded by her), I have enrolled to study law at her alma mater. We have a child on the way and a romance filled with love and laughter. Whenever I sweet-talk her in English, it always makes her giggle: she finds my intonation amusing. She says it is the way I stress my vowels when I speak, as if I am speaking in Hausa, and how I do not use contractions. She would rather I not call her honey, sugar, darling, sweetie, or baby. But what other loving terms of address remain? She says I should just call her by her name, or call her 'Safi', which many of her friends in this country pronounce 'Sophie', thinking it is an English name. Well, at least I pronounce 'Safiya' better than the British.

Little Gods

Part One: Heaven on Earth

Moji clutched her diary and inched barefoot across the patio over-looking the driveway, loving the cold feel of the marble floor against her soles. Sooner or later, she would have to sink her feet into the icky, rain-wetted lawn. Just like it was two nights ago, the rain had turned the lagoon into a curious gem, a jewel that mirrored the moon's shine. Moji was tired of poring over it from the first floor of Lara's two-storey Lekki Beach home, tired of wondering what hid beyond its emerald glitters. She came out to the front yard with a good feeling she would stumble upon a secret path to it—perhaps a dust road lit up by fireflies that went straight through the brick wall.

Every day she wrote in her diary. It was a habit she developed over the last twenty years or so, something she started doing to support facts she might one day begin to doubt, or no longer remember, her way of talking to herself in times when she had no-one to talk to. Her lonely days were getting lonelier as her widowhood stretched by the year.

The three moons of the trident lamp post loomed in the driveway. There were dark patches on each globe and the globes made a crackling noise. Moji felt something land on her neck and slapped at it. She looked up and saw—winged insects: locusts, hundreds of them. Swarming around the globes, drawn to the light, looking like dark patches where they settled, their wings sounding together in crackles and pops.

Shakily, she opened her diary to her last entry, took out her diary pen, and with one hand, raised her diary to the light. A few locusts fell on the pages she held apart by the spine while she wrote:

How time flies. How long has it been? Sixty-four? —no, sixty-five years. Sixty-five years since the day I first laid eyes on Taiwo. I was with him for only fourteen years, fourteen wondrous years, yet it still feels like he's been with me my whole life.

Lara no longer entertained any talk about Taiwo. Ever since Femi died, almost ten years ago, Lara seemed to resent her for still thinking about the boy she loved before she loved her father. How could she choose to dwell on her jilt instead of a husband who had loved her for forty years and three months? It wasn't fair to Femi, true. But it wasn't something Moji could help. She couldn't deny it: what she shared with Taiwo was rare. It was unheard of. Taiwo was the love of her life. And you can only have one love of your life. So of course, she missed him more. Yes, Femi had loved her dearly and had always been good to her, but Taiwo was her twin soul. You can't compete with that. Back when Lara was younger, Moji's teen romance had been their mother-daughter secret, their special bond. It wasn't a secret. Not really. Femi had known about Taiwo. He just never knew how strongly Moji felt about him, or that she never stopped thinking about him.

The last time she and Lara spoke about Taiwo, Lara had shocked her when she said, "I thought they were fairy tales, Mama, just a love story you made up for me when I was young."

Taiwo? A made-up story? Why would she do that? Why would she fabricate a love story for her daughter and put herself in it?

"When you said both of you could... you know... Heal each other with a touch. Were you speaking metaphorically?" Lara asked, and Moji had replied with a firm 'no.'

"Oh, Mama," Lara had said. "I don't know what to think. But please, I beg you. Let's give Taiwo a rest for now. It's only been two months since Daddy died."

Lara was now forty-two and a pediatrician. She worked at Macaulay Memorial, a private hospital in Lagos mainland. For years, she had insisted on Moji coming to live with her, with her and her daughter Yemisi. Eventually, Moji did. She relocated to Lagos, to Lara's beach home in the Lekki peninsula. It wasn't because she needed taking care of, but because she wanted to help Lara get through a painful divorce.

Standing at the edge of the patio, Moji put a leg forward and carefully, sank her foot into the grass, and water pooled around it. She squelched across the driveway and a dark shape running towards her gave her a start. The shape was rubbed against her legs and wagged its tail. It was Simi, Lara's poodle. She reached down and patted her furry little head. The lamp post in front of the house didn't illuminate the entire driveway. Or maybe it was her cataract making everything darker than it was.

"Mama," she heard a voice call. It sounded like Lara. "I'm here," the voice said.

A wide-hipped, big-thighed silhouette of a moderately tall woman (Lara in trousers) rose from her crouch and waved a big hand at Moji. Lara was in her little garden roundabout. Her hands looked massive. It was only until she took them off that Moji realized they were a gardening gloves.

"Going somewhere?" Lara asked.

"Not really. Just want to feel the damp soil between my toes, that's all. Is my granddaughter back from school?"

"She's been back a long time. She said you were sleeping and she didn't want to wake you. She's in the children's parlor doing her homework."

"Alright then." Moji turned to go back into the house. "Mama?"

"Yes."

"About Yemisi. I've been wanting to talk to you about her." Lara came into the light. "Mama, don't take this the wrong way, but I don't want you putting ideas in her head."

"What ideas?"

"You told her about the Ibeji when she came home yesterday, didn't you?"

"It was for her Social Studies homework. She said her class was asked to write about the ancient practices of the Yoruba and she asked me if I had witnessed the killing of twins. I said no, but I was aware it was happening at the time. I didn't tell her about that bit of history. They teach that in schools these days."

"But you said more than that didn't you, Mama? You know what? Forget it. Forget I brought it up."

"No, tell me. What did I say?"

Lara was silent for a moment before she said, "You told her twin souls, and not twins per se, was what people were afraid of back then. She said you said people were scared of them because they were like heaven on earth, too perfect for our world. She said you said that their existence upset the natural cycle of reincarnation and, ultimately, the essence of creation.

Moji sighed. She had rambled on that evening.

"The natural cycle of reincarnation, Mama? Do we practise Ifa now? If you're a traditionalist, then let me make it clear to you that I want to raise my daughter a Christian."

"I said that only after she asked me why twins were killed. I wasn't the one who told her about the killing of twins. They teach that in schools these days."

Lara made a guttural sound. "Mama, I don't care."

"I didn't tell her that I'm a twin soul myself or that I've met my other half if that's what you're worried about."

Lara gave her a look that mourned her and returned to her gardening. She didn't say another word.

Moji rubbed her eyelids and squeezed out tears. Taiwo, look what you've done to me: everyone thinks I'm crazy. Why did you come into my life? Why?

Taiwo was a boy she first met at the hospital where her mother was being treated for fibroids. As her mother didn't like the food there, every morning she took breakfast to her before she left for school. Taiwo was not like most of the other in-patients. He wasn't bed-ridden. Or sickly. In fact, he seemed quite well, well enough to play Hide And Seek and explore the hospital for the fun of discovering things. She was eleven at the time and he was thirteen. Even now, she could still see him rolling around in the grass and laughing as he recalled the private remonstrations of a cook they caught talking to herself, thinking no-one was watching. It was then that she had asked him the question that was foremost on her mind.

They muffle their laughter and crawl away, keeping their heads below the kitchen's window sill. They scurry to the big mango tree near the laundry, support for one end of a washing line, and Taiwo slumps on the ground and cackles.

Moji watches him for a while, grinning, and then she asks, "Are you sick? You seem quite well to me."

"I have appendicitis," he says. "What's that?"

"It's when food gets trapped here." He points to the right side of his belly, a little above his waistline.

"Does it hurt?"

"Only when you press it."

"Like this?" She jabs him in the ribs and he flinches, twisting his body away from her.

"Don't," he blurts. After a while, he says, "Funny. I didn't feel a thing. Touch me there again."

She pokes him in the same spot and this time he doesn't budge. He asks her to do it again. And again. And again. Each time, he wrinkles his brow, looking more confused. Finally, she pinches him and he yells.

The next day, she learns Taiwo has been discharged. A week passes. Eventually, her mother is discharged and she concludes she has seen the last of him. But three days later, while she is making her way home from school, squealing and laughing with her friends, she hears someone call her name and she spins around. It's Taiwo. He is not alone. There is a tall slim man with him. The man has an afro with a side part, and sideburns, and moves with the aid of a walking cane.

"Taiwo," she screams and stops short of hugging him. "You're here. Are you a new pupil?"

"No. I came to find you."

"Me? How did you know I was here?"

He laughs. "Have you forgotten I asked you what school you went to and you told me? Well." He gloats. "I didn't forget."

Moji notices her friends waiting for her by a stationery stall and waves them goodbye, and they leave.

"Is she the one?" the man asks Taiwo. "Yes, Papa," Taiwo says.

The one who what? Moji wonders. Remembering her manners, she greets the elderly man in Yoruba and bows before him.

"Young girl, do you know what you did?" the man says. Moji doesn't know what to make of his expression. Is he upset or is he pleased? And what did she do?

"No," she says, looking at Taiwo.

"You cured me," Taiwo says.

"Cured who? You? I didn't do anything."

The man flags down an ice-cream vendor on a bicycle and buys two ruby-red ice-lollies, one for Taiwo and one for Moji.

Moji thanks the elderly man.

"Meet my father," Taiwo says.

"Call me Baba Kayode," the man says to her.

They move away from the mammy market. They head towards the shade under a big mango tree beside a provisions store. They sit under the tree and Taiwo and Moji lick their ice-lollies in silence. Baba Kayode gives Moji sporadic glances. He smiles at her when she catches him a second time. Moji makes up her mind to turn down whatever reward they might offer her, certain she is not deserving.

When they finish eating their lollies, Baba Kayode asks Taiwo to show Moji his scar. Taiwo unbuttons his shirt. He has a coarse fold of darker skin on the left side of his chest, above his nipple. It's a burn.

"I don't remember how I got it," Taiwo says.

"He was four," Baba Kayode says to Moji. "His mother left him by the cooking fire to attend to other things." He points to the burn. "Touch him there."

Moji hesitates. They wait.

She palms it. She spreads her fingers apart and rubs. Not knowing what else to do to satisfy their curiosities, she keeps rubbing. Taiwo moans and asks her not to stop.

She rubs until she begins to feel the weight of her arm. Fortunately, Baba Kayode asks her to remove her hand.

When she pulls her hand away, the burn is... gone. Gone without a trace. She gasps.

No-one offers her an explanation. Baba Kayode rolls up his trouser and asks her to touch his shin.

She obliges him.

"I don't feel anything," he says to Taiwo.

He asks Moji to stop and start again. She scrubs his shin with both hands.

"Still nothing," the man says with his eyes closed. "Now both of you hold hands. Taiwo, you touch my leg."

Moji and Taiwo do as he says. It takes a few minutes, but he soon begins to rock back and forth like someone in a trance. When Taiwo stops waxing his leg, he stretches it and stares at it. Carefully, he puts his foot down, stands on both feet, and begins to hop on that leg, laughing and singing praises in Yoruba.

Moji was not sure of it now, but when she first met Baba Kayode, he may have had tribal marks—three long lines that stretched from the corners of his mouth to his temples. She can't remember that far back vividly, but she was sure she and Taiwo had used their synergy to transform his face, whether it was to strengthen his facial bones, fix his teeth, or remove tribal marks.

EVERY FRIDAY, Moji came to Macaulay Memorial Hospital, hoping perchance she would meet a certain someone from her past. It was rather optimistic of her, she knew, still, it was better than nothing. The nurses at the reception had grown tired of her asking them to go through their patient roster for a 'Taiwo Kolawole Adetokunbo'.

"Have you tried the mortuary?" a rude middle-aged matron said to her.

But Taiwo couldn't be dead. If he was, how could she still feel his life force pulsing through her? She was seventy-seven, so he would be seventy-nine, and even though their hearts were beating considerably slower now, it seemed the strength of their heartbeats were combining to produce palpitations unlikely for people their age.

MRS. FELICIA MAKATA WAS ALREADY IN THE CHAPEL when Moji entered. Felicia was a woman in her sixties. She came very often to the chapel to pray. She came every weekday, after dropping her husband off for his weekly chemotherapy. She avoided people, especially those she knew, anyone who wasn't hospital staff. She seemed to avoid widows even more—they were not the company she wanted to keep. Moji thought she saw her overtures as a sort of co-optation into a sisterhood of widows, and she didn't want that. She became more tolerant towards Moji after overhearing a nurse address Moji as 'Iya Dokita' (Doctor's mother).

Moji knelt beside her and fixed her eyes on the altar, on the brass monstrance shaped like the sun and its rays. They were the only ones in the chapel. She said a short prayer and whispered to Felicia, "Can I tell you a secret?"

Felicia neither spoke nor gave her a sign that she had heard. "Once upon a time, I could heal people with a touch." Felicia wound sideways to look at her.

"I lost it," Moji said.

"That must have been very hard on you," Felicia said.

Moji had expected her to ask her how she lost it and not patronize her. It was how a skeptic would respond. "I lost him. That's why I lost it," Moji volunteered. "I ended up marrying the wrong guy. That's why I can't anymore." She sighed. Now, even she thought she sounded crazy.

Felicia returned to her meditation. She didn't ask. Moji couldn't blame her; she was equally disbelieving herself when Taiwo proposed. When he proposed they marry—other people.

Bosom friends since the day Baba Kayode made them realize what they were, their union was like the spit they spat into each other's bruises, a balm that healed and renewed them. They complemented each other. They improved and sustained each others' bodies and souls. They went through puberty together like two seedlings on a farm with enough manure. They blossomed into perfect specimens, healthy and beautiful, their bodies the right shape and proportion. People told Moji she looked like her mother in the form of an angel. Naturally, eventually, they caved into their lust. Moji never knew she was capable of such undisguised hunger. She wanted him in her, wanted him every single day, in every single way. The end of every orgasm marked the beginning of a new one or the promise of one. Every smile he gave, every gesture he made, every teeny show of affection, propelled her into a vortex of longing that could only be doused by another orgasm. It was an addiction she didn't want to give up.

The first time he filled her, she was fourteen. She had collapsed on top of him and they had fallen asleep 'like two snakes sleeping through the dry season', that was how Baba Kayode described them. They were out for hours. Worried, after banging on the door and getting no answer, Baba Kayode had burst in and woken them. He could have said something then, but he didn't, he left it for them to figure out. Eventually, they did.

That moment came in 1958, at St. Stephen's Comprehensive Grammar School, Akure. Moji was in her penultimate year at the school and Taiwo was in his final year. It was Prep Time and they were alone in a classroom studying when Moji, after reading her mother's letter, shared the good news that her old aunt was finally getting married. Their conversation took an awry turn after Moji said she was looking forward to her wedding and Taiwo siad he couldn't say the same. Shocked, Moji forgot about being coy and asked him if he wasn't excited about starting a family with her.

"Moji, I think it would be best if we married other people," Taiwo says.

Moji studies his expression and realizes he isn't joking. "What do you mean 'marry other people'?" she asks.

"You're shouting," he says. "Can you lower your voice, please?" He scampers over desks and benches to get to the classroom door and closes it. Still not satisfied, he shuts all the windows too.

The windows are shutters made of metal with three small slits for ventilation. (They're metallic to keep students from breaking them.) The classroom is dark now, even though it's sunny outside. Moji is oblivious to her rapid breathing. She is only aware of Taiwo, who is like a metal window himself, opaque and inscrutable, depriving her of sun and air.

He looks at her staidly and says, "You know what we are."

"Taiwo, you're scaring me. I am not the reincarnation of your late twin sister."

"How would you even know that? But even if you're not Kehinde, you are my soul, the part of me that completes me. We are perfect together."

"Yes. We are. Perfect together. Is that so bad?"

"Moji, listen to me. We must find perfection on our own, like everyone else. There will be no heaven for us unless we are deemed worthy, separately."

"And we will. We are still two very different people."

"If we marry, we will always have each other to touch and heal. We will always be healthy and never grow old and die. And if we never die, how can we cross to the other side, like everyone else? We'll be stranded here forever. My father says we won't even have children."

"Why won't we have children?"

"Because we would be starting a new race, a race heaven doesn't approve of. For as long as we're together, we will always be beautiful, but we'll be barren too, my dad says."

"I don't care."

"For God's sake, Moji, we may never die. The only way we will is if one of us is fatally wounded and dies before the other can get to him, or her. When our mates are eighty, we'll still be looking like this. That's when everyone will know we shouldn't be here."

"No," she screams and covers her ears. Her heart pleads for him to stop talking.

"Moji, we need to live apart so we can fall sick and die, like everyone else. We can't keep living in our own little heaven. This is not our place."

"Can you really say goodbye? To me?"

He looks her straight in the eye and waits a while before he says, "As long as one heart beats, the other will feel it. We will always be in each other's heart for as long as we live."

"But I can't… I don't want to live without you. Taiwo, I love you so much."

"And I love you too. You're my life. But I must make you my other life, not this one. I take comfort in knowing, ahead of time, whom I will be spending eternity with. I have you to look forward to, Moji, and when that time comes, we won't have anything to fear because we won't be… different."

"You say 'different' like it's a bad thing. If anything, I feel special, like a little god. Don't you like healing those in our prayer group whenever we all hold hands and form a circle?"

"Yes, but if they knew it was us, our lives won't be the same. The Ifa teaches that wherever people like us are found, they should kill one and leave the other. That's how to make it right." He lowers his head and adds," that's what they did to Kehinde."

There were tears in his voice even though Moji knew he could not remember his sister: he was almost two when she was taken.

Moji hugs Taiwo. They cry in each other's arms and dry each other's eyes. From the core of her being, Moji swears never to leave him, never to let go, no matter what. She can tell he's conflicted; his heart feels the same but he's too afraid to listen to it. But Taiwo will disappear from her life and she will learn that Baba Kayode has sent him off to a university whose identity no-one knows, or is willing to tell her. A decade will pass and Taiwo will not return. All she will be left with (to remind her he was not something she imagined) is a heart awake to his life force.

Part Two: Drums of Oubala

Bumblebees fluttered and fussed over hibiscuses before settling on them. Moji rocked in her garden chair, jerking awake between naps, and finally waking when she whiffed cigarette fumes and coughed. Where was it coming from? Who could be smoking? Could it be Kunle the cook? He had better not be smoking in the house. The way the capricious wind blew, it was hard to tell where the smoke was coming from. She peeled her back from her chair and looked around for the source. There was no-one about. So she sneaked into the house through the kitchen, hoping to catch the culprit red-handed.

The fumes of smoke were coming from the parlor. They grew stronger as she approached. On the long couch. With her back to the kitchen was... Lara? Or someone that looked like her. No. It was her. She was home early. She massaged her neck muscles with both hands and then she picked up a cigarette and held it to her ear. Lara? Smoking? But she said she quit.

Moji shuffled into the room, dragging her feet on the ground so it announced her. Lara glanced up at her and returned to flaking off the butt of her cigarette into an ashtray next to an empty champagne bottle.

"Didn't know you were home," Moji said.

Lara tilted her head and blew a puff of smoke in the air, the bangs on her weave-on falling away from her eyes.

Moji coughed. "Do you want to be by yourself?" Lara didn't reply so Moji made to leave.

"I think something's wrong with me?" Lara said. "What?"

"I don't know exactly."

Moji took the couch opposite Lara's.

"Okay, I admit. I've had my suspicions." She cast another dragon's breath of white clouds. "My only child is nearly sixteen, and I've not been able to get pregnant since. It was what cost me my marriage."

"Well, good riddance to Tosin. May he find the biological child he is looking for."

"But that's not what's bothering me, Mama. I learned something today."

Moji waited.

"I had an emergency this morning," Lara said, staring blankly at the coffee table. "An accident victim, a little boy. He needed B-positive blood and we had none left in the bank, but lucky for him I'm B-positive."

"So you gave him blood."

"It had to be screened first. When the results came back, they said it wasn't fresh."

"Really?"

"What nonsense, I thought. How could it be? I drew it myself, right there in my office. They must have mixed it up with someone else's. So I drew another pint from my vein and checked it myself."

"And?"

"They were right. It was stale." Lara froze. The cigarette she shoved between her lips fell to the rug. "I apologized to the lab and lied that I had made a mistake; I was AB-positive."

"You're just learning this now? After all the fertility tests?"

Lara stared at Moji, looking a little fazed by her reaction and then looking past her. "I shouldn't be alive, Mama. In case you don't know, it isn't possible for the blood of a living, breathing human being to be stale. My cells have low ATP concentrations. If I were crazy, I would say I have rigor mortis and that I was dead."

"Can I tell you a story?"

"Please, Mama. This isn't the time."

"Suit yourself. But remember, I tried to tell you."

Lara saw the cigarette she had dropped smouldering into her rug and quickly stamped it out. She sank back on her couch and gave Moji a long hard stare.

"It had better not have anything to do with Taiwo," she said.

"But it does."

"Are you going to tell me that he's my real father and that I'm some sort of miracle birth? Because I've had it with you and your supernatural lover?"

"No, he is not your father."

"Does it have anything to do with twin souls and people who can heal each other with a touch?"

"Do you want to hear the truth or not?"

Lara pursed her lips.

"Remember the time we went to Porto-Novo?" Moji said. "Yemisi was three then, and we left her with your father and your grandmother. I had suggested you come with me because I thought you could use a break from motherhood, and a holiday from men as well, after Yemisi's father—what's that boy's name again? —turned out to be married and a big fat liar."

"You were doing your masters at the time and you said you wanted me to come along with you to help you with your anthropology paper, which was on Voodoo and the people of Benin."

"I lied, I'm sorry. There was no paper. Voodoo had fascinated me for years; it was the closest thing I knew to what I shared with Taiwo. I hoped I would learn something useful from our trip."

THE SUN PEAKS OVER JARDIN VACANCES, a seaside resort in the port city of Porto-Novo. Moji, Lara, and six other tourists crowd around Bayor the guide and stare up a hillock: Mount Egun, they're told it's called, taking mental notes of the steep climb it presents. Encouraged by the news that their trek was nearing its end, Moji looks for cracks to fit her fingers and pull herself up, but Bayor beats her to it and scrambles to the top of the hillock. He secures a rope around the trunk of a kapok tree and throws down the other end. One-by-one, the eight of them strap it on like a body harness, and he hauls them up.

On the other side, there is a dilapidated building with a long veranda and a much-corroded zinc roof basking in the purple gas-flare of the evening sun.

"Is this where Oubala lives?" Lara asks Bayor.

"This is our tollgate," he says. "This is where you will pay for your passage. Koroma, our keeper, will attend to all of you."

Moji frowns. "You mean…? We've only just reached your toll gate?" Bayor chuckles. "Don't worry. Oubala's place is not far from here. Please wait here, all of you, while I go and inform Koroma that you have arrived." He canters down the slope, to the building below, and disappears behind a curtained door.

"I wonder what they do with all the money they collect," Jean-Pierre, one of two French tourists, says, looking at the ramshackle building Bayor had entered.

"Yeah," Jeremy, an American tourist, says. "This is a wilderness. I bet 'a keeper' is what they call a ranger here."

Their guide returns with Koroma the Keeper. The Keeper is wearing long baggy shorts and knee-length stockings. He looks like a school principal in the colonial era. He speaks fluent English. After introducing himself, he says, "China gave the world acupuncture, but Benin gave her something even better: Voodoo. Welcome to Voodoo's holiest site."

He informs them that at the stroke of midnight, drums will sound to stir up spirits of the dead and that they will be expected to be ready to meet Oubala. He warns that Oubala takes offence when people run from him, as a few sometimes do, and so if they wish to be tied-up when they see him, it would be a wise choice.

"Why do they run from him?" someone asks.

"The person you will see is unsightly," The Keeper says. "Since he takes upon himself the afflictions of others, he is expectedly hideous. If you have full-blown AIDS, his vicarious touch will cure you. Unfortunately for him, he will contract it, and all the other diseases you have. You transmit. Oubala receives. That's the way it is."

"Amazing," Smithie, the big Aussie, says. "And he's still alive, is he?"

"I don't know," the Keeper says. "People say he is a zombie. And if that is true, it means he is already dead. Now, I hope you all came with cash. We don't take cheques or credit cards."

"Did you hear that?" Lara mutters to Moji. "Oubala the great healer is a real-life zombie."

Jean-Pierre, who is pacing between tourists, stops to say, "Not real-life. Real dead. Real-dead zombie." He fleers at Lara and saunters off.

Bayor describes Oubala as a hermit who is likely to repulse with his appearance and urges everyone to choose the option of being tied when they are laid out on his altar. Moji doesn't fancy this idea.

"I wonder where we'll sleep," Rick Matthews, another American, says, speaking Moji's mind.

"After seeing Oubala, I don't think any of us will sleep," Jean-Pierre says and horselaughs in Rick's face.

Bayor, walking ahead of them, takes them to an airy slope with fig trees. "You can rest here," he says.

With their backs on the ground and their heads pillowed by their knapsacks, Moji says to Lara, "You're not going. You'll wait for me here."

"But I am," Lara says. "We can see him together if you like, the two of us."

"This is my research. It is not your call."

"Well, I didn't come all this way just to carry your bags. I'm going. I'm not eager to see a zombie, true, which is why I'd much rather go with you, but if you aren't fine with that..."

"Lara, please. I have a good mind to forfeit everything and go back to the hotel this very minute."

"And miss out on your healing? Where will you even find a taxi at this hour?"

Moji tries to discourage her, but it's futile. "Fine. We'll go together," she says.

At a quarter to midnight, some locals start a campfire and at the stroke of midnight, they begin to beat hourglass-shaped drums, dunduns, the Drums of Oubala, Bayor says they're called. The thrumming against leather, the chirping of crickets, and the low growls of the wind create an eerie atmosphere. Even Jean-Pierre no longer makes wisecracks. Moji tries again to reason with Lara, but she remains adamant.

They sprawl out on the grass and listen to the distant screams of the first ones to see Oubala. If their screams are anything to go by, Oubala is very frightful. Lara looks tense. She and Moji swap looks.

"Where are the others? Why aren't they coming back after their healing?" Moji asks Bayor.

"From Oubala's altar, they are taken to a place where they can rest and heal completely: our very own African spa if you like. Don't be afraid, madam. Oubala is not a wild animal."

"It is better this way," Jean-Pierre says to Moji. "If they return and tell us what they saw, or how they are feeling afterward, some of us will not want to go."

It is exactly what Moji was hoping would dissuade Lara.

Bayor informs Moji and Lara that they are next, and they, like those before them, follow the Keeper into the deep plains. They walk a considerable distance until they reach a bonfire. Next to it is a tent decorated with cow horns, tortoise shells, and other curios often used as talismans. The fire is a warming presence that changes direction with the wind, like a wrapper batting in the breeze. The night cloaks everything beyond a certain radius in pitch-blackness. Locusts, swarms of them—or whatever they are—fly around it. The Keeper pokes a long stick inside the tent, checking to see if it's empty. Satisfied that it is, he orders them to lie flat on their backs, and then he asks them, for the umpteenth time, if they would like to be tied up. Moji says no and he leaves them with a warning: 'Be still. Scream if you want. But be very still at all times. Oubala could get violent if you flinch.' Moji doesn't like his tone of voice or this latest revelation. Why did he leave it so late to tell them Oubala could be dangerous?

The drums thrum out a different rhythm. The flame crackle with flying insects dart. Lara sniffles. She's crying.

Moji feels around her for Lara's hand and finds her wrist. "Lara, shut your eyes, you hear me."

"They're closed."

"Good. Now keep them that way and don't move no matter what."

Moji hears the thudding of feet. She hears someone chanting a tune, shuffling, dancing from the sound of it. The air smells bad. It gets worse as the sound nears. The sound stops. Moji tenses. She arches her spine and waits. She wants to get up and look around but fears she might not be able to control her reaction when she sees Oubala. She might scream and send Lara on a panic run.

Something coarse rests on her left foot. It's a hand. A palm. It feels callused. Like a foot (but toes can't spread and grasp like fingers). The hand slithers up her left thigh and stops at her stomach. The halitosis she inhales alerts her to the presence of a head just above hers. She glimpses teeth, two sets of gums, one above the other, inches apart. Something thick and wet sloshes on her face. She opens her eyes and sees a long dribble of saliva hanging over her. She twists her head away, partly from the halitosis hitting hard. She reaches up and clasps the head by the ears. She hopes for some synergy to relieve her joint pains and the weakness in her bones, her post-menopausal fatigue.

A sudden surge of energy drains from her and jumpstarts her heart.

The head reels back and makes a deep grating sound like a ram with its throat being slit. It frees itself from her grasp.

In the light of the fire, a thin man in a breechcloth rolls on the ground, coughing. Lara is still lying motionless on her mat. Her eyes are shut but her eyelids are quivering. The strange man has sores all over his body. The flesh on his face has swellings like the bubbles on the surface of a bowl of broth. In place of eyebrows, he has two asymmetrical scar tissues. He trembles on the ground like an epileptic, the scars and the boils on his face shrinking in size. His claw foot resets. His seizure stops and he sits up. He spits and wipes his drooling mouth. He reaches into his breechcloth and pulls out a dagger. Moji scrambles to her feet, surprised at the ease with which she manages this.

The man holds the curved dagger by the hilt and points its tip downwards, ready to stab with a quick motion. Moji wants to yell 'Lara get up and run', but doesn't want to draw attention to Lara until the creature is far enough. She bends down, grabs a fistful of earth, and waits.

The man rushes forward and she throws the sand in his eyes. He shrieks and staggers forward, blinded. He continues in a straight line, moving in the wrong direction. The drums pulsate. He feels around for her with one arm stretched in front of him. She taps him on the back and he spins around, blinking. She taps him again from a different angle, and he follows. Circling and tapping, she leads him towards the fire, bidding her time for the moment when she will shout 'Lara open your eyes and run'. He swings at the air haphazardly. He swerves and turns, anticipating her taps from the back. His movement is too erratic, too frenzied, and too random to predict. He heads in one direction, swings around, and starts in the opposite. He veers towards Lara. It's too risky to try to tap him now, Moji knows. She watches helplessly as he trips over Lara, lands on top of her, and reacts like an ant lion. He shakes her violently. Lara howls. Blood pools onto the sand, spreading like tides on a shore—Lara's blood. Moji screams. She tries to. But she has lost her voice. The drumming stops and Lara's cries fill the night. Moji pulls Oubala off Lara, surprised at her strength and surprised that the creature is rather weak for a man. Oubala, smeared in blood from the waist down, stumbles off into the night like a child afraid of the punishment coming.

Lara's words are incoherent. She gurgles blood. Moji cradles her and uses her hand to plug up the stab wound just below the rib cage. She screams for help and this time, sound leaves her. She can hear running feet.

Moji is trotting behind four men who have wrested Lara from her arms and are carrying her spread-eagle like a carcass.

Moji is in a car with strangers who are driving Lara to hospital.

Moji is in a hallway, striding beside nurses who are wheeling Lara to a theatre in a gurney.

Moji is waiting outside the operating theatre. People in white lab coats scuttle in and out of double-swing doors. Moji hears the words 'We're sorry, madam, but she lost too much blood. We did the best we could.'

Day breaks. Moji has not slept a wink. She can hear the voices of sympathizers. In the stillness of her heart, their words create a soundtrack like the drums of Oubala. They have grown tired of trying to get her to talk.

A mortician is giving her the cost of Lara's embalming, but she is not listening. She is listening to a conversation another man is having with the chief mortuary attendant. The man wants to buy unclaimed bodies for the medical school where he lectures, says he wants to use them as cadavers. His voice sounds familiar but she does not care to look up. He stops talking. She's not sure but she thinks she can feel his eyes. He calls her by her name.

Taiwo? Can it be? He has a beard now. He's bald too. There are small 'tea bags' underneath his eyes. He's not as handsome as she remembers. He stares at her. "Is everything okay?" he asks. "Moji, what's the matter?" She slouches in her chair to avert his eyes. His question makes her realize she's crying. Her tears want to flow, but she doesn't want to do it in front of him. And so she bolts off. She careers down the hallway. She pushes past anyone in her way, brushing away her tears.

She sprints down an arcade free of people. On a long straight, Taiwo catches her and pulls her to him. She sobs in his arms.

"My life is not going well," she says. "Please, let's run off together. We can start over. We can be young again."

"Moji, tell me what happened?" he says.

"I'm a bad mother."

It is hard but she manages to speak about her midnight of madness. He listens. He doesn't judge her. He hugs her tighter and lets her cry some more. Afterward, he tells her about his life.

He is a Professor of Human Anatomy at Sainte Felicite University, where he graduated. He said he had studied Voodoo out of curiousness and it wasn't until he realized he had made a life out of examining corpses, first as an anatomy student and then as a voodoo novitiate, that he decided to be an anatomy lecturer. Moji asks him the questions that still bother her even after all these years: Why did he suddenly leave? Did he not love her anymore? He says he came to Benin to have a life that did not include her, not because he doesn't love her, but because it was for the best. He is not married, he says, and when she asks him why he smiles and says, "Moji, we're about to do something we have never done before."

She discovers what he means when he takes her back to the city, to his lab in the university, where they join hands together and place them over Lara's knife wound.

Part Three: Love and Let Die

THE FESTIVITIES WERE OVER. Moji and her sisters bid the guests goodbye. While several youths took down the canopies and gathered the plastic seats, they settled into hammock chairs to reflect on Yemisi's traditional wedding, the event they had just witnessed.

"She was the most beautiful bride ever. The groom too," Bukola said, leaning into her chair.

Moji nodded. "Isn't it amazing how time flies, how quickly children grow? When we last saw, she wasn't even born."

"Will you be going back with Omolara? Back to Lagos?" Abiola asked Moji.

"I will."

"When?"

"I don't know. Lara hasn't said."

Abiola gave Moji's hand a small squeeze. "You should stay with us."

"Yes, you should," Bidemi said. "The city is too dangerous for you to move around freely. But here, all you have to look out for are bicycles and motorcycles."

Moji sighed. Heavenly is how she would describe the simple rural pleasures she now realized she missed. Like how the clucks of chickens and the low voices of the early risers warmed her heart when she heard them in the morning. Or the way goats and other farm animals behaved like house pets and did not run away from you because they didn't think you could harm them. She had certainly missed her sisters and their gossip.

"Lara still needs me," she said. "We have no husbands, as you already know. And after what you have just seen, Yemisi is about to leave us. But I will think about it."

"Oh. I just remembered something," Abiola said. "Your old boyfriend is back."

"Taiwo? When?"

"Last month, I think."

"He doesn't go out much, they say, so hardly anyone sees him."

"Who is Taiwo?" Bukola asked.

Abiola and Bidemi giggled.

"There was someone else in Moji's life before your brother," Abiola said to Bukola. "Moji was once every man's dream. Don't you remember how beautiful she looked at her wedding? Or did you think Femi was her first?"

"Thank you for the news about Taiwo," Moji said and tried to change the topic. (Yes, she had not been a virgin bride, but it was not something you bragged about.) She tried, but Abiola would not be distracted.

Abiola recalled how Moji and Taiwo had once been the envy of all, and Moji learned in the course of her story that she and Taiwo had been caught stark naked and asleep in each other's arms.

"She was never punished or cautioned," Abiola said. "Till this day, I still don't know why. I think mother liked Taiwo. He was so handsome, my God."

"Did mother see us?" Moji asked, suddenly wanting to know.

Abiola grinned. "No. It was Aunty Abosede who told us what she and Aunty Funmi had seen while working on their farm. We didn't tell Father. Aunty Abosede said the two of you were asleep for hours. If I'm not mistaken, I think Mother and Father quarreled that night."

"What about?"

"I think she wanted father to start treating her better."

"Whatever happened to you guys?" Bukola asked Moji. "You seemed like the perfect couple."

"That's what we'd all like to know," Abiola said. "She didn't say much then. Perhaps she will now."

Moji shrugged. "Taiwo moved across the border, to Benin Republic, and I moved on with my life. End of story."

"You still haven't said anything," Bidemi said.

"Yes," Abiola agreed. "It doesn't make sense. Why would he leave just like that, and never come back for you?"

THAT NIGHT, AFTER BEDTIME PRAYERS, Moji told Lara, Yemisi, and Jide (Yemisi's husband after traditional marriage rites) that she had something to tell them.

"I heard this evening, from my sisters, that Taiwo is back in the country," she said.

Yemisi sat up straight. "He's here?"

"Not here. In Abese, his village. It's not far from here."

"That's great news," Yemisi said. "We can all go to see him and invite him to the church wedding. Do you think he'll come to Lagos?"

"I don't know," Moji said, looking at Lara. "I think I should go alone."

"Nonsense," Lara said. "I'm dying to meet the man who saved my life."

Never in a billion years did Moji think she'd hear those words—from Lara. So she believed? She finally believed. And from the look of it, she had forgiven her too. Moji bent her head over her table, clasped her hands over her forehead to shade her eyes, and cried. She convulsed as she cried quietly. Lara and Yemisi came to cuddle her and fared no better the minute they wrapped their arms around her.

Lara did not have stale blood running through her veins from the tests she conducted privately. What happened was, when even a single drop of her blood left her body, it immediately turned stale. She had found this too bizarre to keep to herself and had shared it with

Moji and Yemisi. Moji surmised that her synergy with Taiwo worked inside her body, but didn't work outside. As for her infertility, Moji said Taiwo had explained to her that their synergy worked through the fusion of their somatic cells. (One of her mono-nuclear cells combined with one of Taiwo's to form a new mono-nuclear cell.) Their healing synergy was the result of new mononuclear cells. Their sex cells never fused and remained unaffected by their synergy. And that was why they could not revive Lara's dead ovaries. Lara had listened quietly while Moji explained all of this. Afterward, she had gotten into her car and gone for a drive. When she returned, later that evening, she went back to her old self and pretended as if they had never had that conversation.

THE SKY WAS THE PEAK OF A GIANT WATERFALL and Abeokuta was its nadir on the day they set out to find Taiwo. The wind was so strong it bounced the boulders that weighted old zinc roofs and skewed the rain as it pissed down. Lightning flashed and thunder crackled. Jide, who was at the wheel, could not see past the concave waves of rain on the windscreen so he turned off the wiper. When his view of the road got even worse, he cleared to the side of the road and parked the car. While they waited for the downpour to subside, a lone Peugeot 504 with its headlamps at full blast blazed past them, drenching their Audi GLS with a splash as high as a market stall. They waited. They had to wait. If not for the rain to stop, for people to come back out. At this juncture, Moji was lost. She needed someone to give them directions on how to get to Taiwo's clan home. Taiwo's town Abese had changed so much from what she remembered.

The rain didn't stop, but the downpour thinned to a drizzle. Dust roads were troughs of mud. Like a master rower, Jide plowed the car through the mire, staying close to the shallower edges. They had the luck of a few pedestrians skirting the mud for directions. Several clans went by the name 'Adetokunbo', so Moji asked if they knew a Kayode Adetokunbo who had a son by the name Taiwo, and they did.

When they reached the place they were told was Taiwo's hamlet, they saw a middle-aged man crouched over some hazelnuts, as he cracked them open with a slate. They asked him which one was Taiwo Adetokunbo's house and he pointed to the white bungalow with a modern design, an oasis in the hamlet. They went up to the door and rang the doorbell. After a few more rings, a young man opened the door slightly and peered at them. He confirmed they were at the right place and then said Taiwo wasn't feeling well and couldn't see visitors. He spoke in a peculiar dialect of Yoruba that Moji knew she had heard somewhere. She groaned when Lara inquired if he was Beninese and he said yes. He introduced himself as Waheed, one of Taiwo's former students, now a medical doctor.

"I hope he is well?" Moji asked.

The young doctor hesitated. "He has prostate cancer," he said.

Lara winced. "How bad is it?"

"Stage four."

Moji's heart sank.

She put on a brave face and tried to appear calm.

She knew her family was watching. "May I see him?" she asked. "He's sleeping at the moment—"

"I would like to see him," she said. "I insist."

Waheed let them in.

Inside, four of Taiwo's kinsmen, three elderly men and a woman, looked up at them from their morose reclinings. Moji asked Lara,

Yemisi, and Jide to wait for her in the hallway while she followed Waheed into Taiwo's bedroom.

The curtains in the room were drawn so they let in just enough light for Moji to make out the shapes of two people: a young woman attending to a catheter and a patient at the end of the catheter. The patient was an old man. He was asleep. He looked in dire need of a shave. He looked starved too. Waheed introduced the woman as Sherifat, his wife, who was also a doctor (another one of Taiwo's students). Moji was a little surprised at her relief, the way her lungs resumed working. She had feared she might be Taiwo's young wife.

"Why is he so thin?" Moji asked.

"He hasn't been eating much," Sherifat said.

"And he refuses to be fed through a tube," Waheed added.

Moji wiped the tears brimming in her eyes. "Thank you," she said. "Both of you. For looking after him."

Their silence asked a question so she said, "I'm Moji, his... his best friend."

Sherifat smiled reassuringly at her and carried on with whatever it was she was doing to the old man.

"I'd like a moment with him. Alone, if you don't mind," Moji said.

Waheed and Sherifat searched each other's faces as they considered her request.

"No problem," Waheed said. "We'll be out in the corridor if you need us."

Moji watched them shuffle out like idlers.

As soon as they shut the door behind them, she brought the old man's hands together over his lap. She paused briefly to examine his face. He was much darker, but he had Taiwo's nose. Still holding his hands, she wondered what to do to wake him; they had to be conscious for them to synergize. And then... she felt him. Not his stir, but his soul. She felt him like a jolt of electricity to her heart, and it was stronger than ever before.

Slowly, his eyes fluttered open, and he squinted at her, trying to make out who she was.

"Moji?" he asked. He yanked his hands away from hers and broke the surge of energy coursing between them.

"If you do it, I will hang myself," he croaked. "And you will have my death on your conscience."

Baffled, she stared at him. He was serious. Like the time he said they should not marry. She felt dizzy. She needed air. It was how she was when she was tense, and she was often tense before she lost her temper.

She took a deep breath to calm herself. "I've missed you," she said. "Missed us." The hoarseness in her voice was gone. Their brief synergy had returned youth to her vocal cords. "My life is the most... painful anyone could have: To experience what completes you and to know that you can never have it. Ever again. I need this, Taiwo. Do it for me, if you won't do it for you. If you love me, do it. Please. We can go back to our old selves, afterwards. I beg you."

He shook his head. "No. Let it go. You need to stop chasing ephemeral happiness. People can get euphoric from taking drugs and alcohol, but their joy never lasts. They won't be truly happy. Is this what you want for us, to live for the next euphoria like addicts?"

"An eternity is made up of several brief moments."

"An eternity where? Here? That can't happen. It shouldn't. I am going to another place to wait for you."

Unable to carry her weight any longer, she lowered herself into the chair beside his bed. "Okay," she said. "Just answer this question for me. How come you never got married?"

He asked her to prop him up with the second pillow beside him, and she helped him up to a small slant and stuck the pillow underneath his back. It made it much easier for him to talk.

"I was married once but she left me. It lasted about a year. The women in my life—the women after you—all complained about the same thing: I seemed far away when I was with them. My wife said she didn't know what to do to make me happy and that made her very unhappy. That was when I told her about you. I left out the synergy, of course. After that, she told me she was leaving, and I said, 'I won't stop you'.

"The truth is, I've always felt like I wasn't meant to be with anyone but you. Always felt that I wasn't—that we weren't meant to be here. That never changed."

Moji was struggling to hold back her tears at this point. She wanted to hit him, but then again, she wanted to kiss him. She tried to form words but could only cry harder. She screamed.

Taiwo's doctors rushed into the room. They must have expected to see his corpse or to see him fighting for his life because they stopped and stared when they saw him propped up on his bed. He motioned them to leave and they retraced their steps and shut the door.

When Moji and Taiwo had been silent long enough, she said to him, "My husband died almost twenty years ago. Liver cirrhosis. He was a heavy drinker. I heard you were back so I came to see you. I came with my family: my daughter, my granddaughter and her husband. My granddaughter just got married the customary way. She's a cartographer. She makes maps for people yet she's still trying to find her way in the world."

He smiled.

"My daughter—you know her—Lara, the one you saved—"

"We saved. We."

"Yes. We. You forget that after so long. Well, she's a pediatrician now." She paused. "I've been meaning to ask you: Is she ever going to die? I sometimes wonder about that."

"She will. After one of us is. With one of us gone, there is no synergy. Everything we've done, everything we've created, goes back to the way it was."

"Are you saying…?"

"Yes."

She allowed it all to sink in and was rather amazed at her response. "Thank you. I needed to know that."

"You're welcome."

"Can you at least stay alive until her daughter is married in church? In a week?"

"I'll try."

"Would you like to meet my family?"

"Sure."

Moji went out into the hallway and ushered Lara, Yemisi, and Jide in. It was the happiest she had ever been in a long time. Finally, they had met Taiwo and he was as real to them as he had ever been to her. But what she would like, if Taiwo would allow, was for them to… Just a small demonstration… For her children.

About the Author

Charles Opara is a Nigerian-born author who writes suspense, speculative fiction, and short stories. He is a programmer with a passion for groundbreaking technologies. His creative mind enjoys the logic involved in writing stories and programs. In 2015, his horror short "It Happened" was shortlisted for the Awele Creative Trust Prize and in 2017, another story 'Baby-girl' was long-listed for the Quramo National Prize in his country. His stories have appeared in Ambit, Flash Fiction Press, and Zoetic Press.

twitter handle: Charles Opara@OparaCc

International Publications

Fake It, Flash Fiction Press
 (http://www.theflashfictionpress.org/2016/06/24/fake-it/)
Fermenting, Zoetic Press
Broken Sleep, Ambit Magazine

Writing Credits

'It Happened' shortlisted for Awele Creative Writers' Prize 2014
'The Dream' longlisted for Fiction Desk's Best Newcomer's Prize 2015
'Fermenting' nominated for the Best of the Net (Zoetic Press 2016)
'Baby-girl' longlisted for the Quramo National Short Story Prize 2017

Fomite

More story collections from Fomite...

MaryEllen Beveridge — *After the Hunger*
MaryEllen Beveridge — *Permeable Boundaries*
Jay Boyer — *Flight*
L. M Brown — *Treading the Uneven Road*
L. M Brown — *Were We Awake*
Michael Cocchiarale — *Here Is Ware*
Michael Cocchiarale — *Still Time*
Neil Connelly — *In the Wake of Our Vows*
Catherine Zobal Dent — *Unfinished Stories of Girls*
Zdravka Evtimova —*Carts and Other Stories*
John Michael Flynn — *Off to the Next Wherever*
Derek Furr — *Semitones*
Derek Furr — *Suite for Three Voices*
Elizabeth Genovise — *Where There Are Two or More*
Andrei Guriuanu — *Body of Work*
Zeke Jarvis — *In A Family Way*
Arya Jenkins — *Blue Songs in an Open Key*
Bobby Johnston — *The Saint I Ain't*
Jan English Leary — *Skating on the Vertical*
Julia MacDonnell— *The Topography of Hidden Stories*
Marjorie Maddox — *What She Was Saying*
William Marquess — *Badtime Stories*
William Marquess — *Because Because Because Because Because*
William Marquess — *Boom-shacka-lacka*
William Marquess — *Things I Want You to Do*
Gary Miller — *Museum of the Americas*
Jennifer Anne Moses — *Visiting Hours*
Martin Ott — *Interrogations*
George Ovitt — *The Showcase*
Christopher Peterson — *Amoebic Simulacra*
Christopher Peterson — *Scratch the Itchy Teeth*
Charles Phillips — *Dead South*
Jack Pulaski — *Love's Labours*
Charles Rafferty — *Saturday Night at Magellan's*
Joseph Rathgeber — *Bad Days on the Batso*
Mohsen Rezaei — *The Violet Needle*
Ron Savage — *What We Do For Love*
Vince Sgambati — *Undertow of Memory*
Fred Skolnik— *Americans and Other Stories*
Lynn Sloan — *This Far Is Not Far Enough*
L.E. Smith — *Views Cost Extra*
Caitlin Hamilton Summie — *To Lay To Rest Our Ghosts*
Susan Thomas — *Among Angelic Orders*

Fomite

Tom Walker — *Signed Confessions*
Silas Dent Zobal — *The Inconvenience of the Wings*

Writing reviews on social media sites for readers will help the progress of independent publishing. To submit a review, go to the book page on any of the sites and follow the links for reviews. Books from independent presses rely on reader-to-reader communications.

For more information or to order any of our books, visit:
http://www.fomitepress.com/our-books.html